Honey

B. WISEMAN

First edition

ISBN 979-8-218-79383-8 (paperback)

Contents

Content Note

Honey is a healing romance rooted in heartbreak, resilience, and rediscovery. This is Lainey's story, a journey of leaving, starting over, and learning that love should never hurt.

Please note: this book contains depictions of emotional, verbal, financial, and physical abuse, including scenes that may be triggering to survivors. Reader discretion is advised.

Featured Tropes:

- Healing from trauma

- Small town setting

- Found family

- Childhood friends turned confidantes

- Ranch life vibes

- Survivors journey

- Domestic violence

- Good girl x bad boy but toxic

- Love bombing

- Sunshine x storm

- Personal growth

- Reclaiming identity

- Empowerment and transformation

- Emotional healing

- New beginnings

- Woman rediscovers herself after an abusive relationship

- Interior designer x Construction worker

- Coffee shop moments

- First love ≠ true love

- Strong female friendships

- Yellow Jeep energy (yes, it's a vibe)

This is not a love story that begins with romance, it begins with survival. But if you're willing to ride through the dust and the dark, there's light on the other side.

A Letter of Thanks

To Avery Anna,

Your album *Breakup over Breakfast* came into my life like a quiet storm, gentle, but deeply felt. Each song carried something real, something raw, but it was *Honey* that stopped me in my tracks. That song became the heartbeat of this book.

There was something about the emotion in *Honey*, the ache, the vulnerability, the strength, that stayed with me long after the music faded. In it, I saw a girl who had lost herself in love, who was learning how to find her way back. That girl became Lainey. That song became her story.

This book is about healing, about choosing yourself even when it's hard, and about rediscovering the parts of you that someone tried to take away. It's a story of quiet courage and it wouldn't exist without *Honey*.

Thank you, Avery, for giving us music that speaks to the parts of us we sometimes forget how to name. Because of your song, *Honey* was born.

With all the gratitude in my heart,

B. Wiseman

Lainey's Playlist

These are the songs that carried Lainey through the silence, the heartbreak, and the healing.

Some of them she cried to.

Some she survived to.

Some she danced to with Lemon in the kitchen with the windows open.

1. **"Bare Minimum" - Jillian Ross**

2. **"The Best" - Rachel Grae**

3. **"Blame It On My Broken Heart" - Avery Anna**

4. **"Break my Bones" - Matt Hansen**

5. **"Breakup over Breakfast" - Avery Anna**

6. **"Devil in Disguise" - Kylie Muse**

22. **"Someone to you"** - Matt Hansen

23. **"Strangers again"** - Matt Hansen

24. **"This is me letting you go"** - Rosie Darling

25. **"Unsaid"** - Jessica Baio

26. **"Where you belong"** - Matt Hansen

27. **"Yardsale"** - Alex Warren

To the girl who stayed when she should have run. Who lost herself trying to make someone else whole. Who thought survival meant silence.

And to anyone who sees themselves in her—this is your reminder that you are so much more than your pain. There is a way out, and on the other side lies a strength you never knew you had. This is for you, because you are worth saving.

Prologue

Once Upon a Whisper

THE SMELL OF BURNT toast clawed at my nose. I didn't even like toast anymore—the way it crunched too loud in my mouth, the butter never melting all the way. Still, I made it. Every morning. One slice, always a little too dark. Toast. coffee. silence. That's what mornings looked like now.

The tile floor chilled my feet, even through the socks I'd pulled from the laundry basket in the living room. I hadn't folded clothes in a week. I didn't care. If Austin noticed, he hadn't said. I kept waiting for the comment—the dig dressed as a joke. He'd find the right moment, slide it in when I wasn't braced for it.

The toaster clicked loudly—I jumped, a reflex. My fingers hovered over the lever a second too long, before I pulled the slice free. The edge was blackened—I scraped at it over the sink, flakes falling like ash. I dropped the toast onto a plate and stared at it.

"You gonna eat it, or just stare at it?" His voice drifted in from the hallway.

I didn't turn. "I'm eating."

"Doesn't look like it."

He stood behind me now. I felt the shift in the air—the heaviness that clung to him when he was in a mood. I tried to gauge it without looking, eyes on the butter knife like it had some kind of answer. My hand moved slowly, spreading the butter—quiet, controlled. No noise. no mess.

He dropped into the chair at the end of the table. It creaked under him. He didn't even like that chair—said it wobbled too much, like it might give out beneath him, and somehow that'd be my fault.

"You drink the last of the milk?"

I nodded. "I'll get more later."

"Right," he muttered, dragging a finger across the table's edge. "Or maybe I'll pick some up, since I'm the only one who ever leaves this house."

I kept my mouth shut, biting back the sharpness that wanted out. My toast went cold while I pretended to care about how the butter refused to spread evenly.

"Seriously," he said, louder. "What do you even do all day?"

I turned just enough to look at him—not fully. He was slouched back, arms crossed, a smirk tugging at his mouth like he was daring me to say something wrong. His hair was still damp from the shower, curling at his jawline. He hadn't shaved in days. I hated how much that used to make him look sexy to me.

"I clean. I cook. I—" I swallowed. "I try to keep things together."

"For who? Me?" He laughed, short and hard. "You think I need you to do all that?"

"No," I said quickly, too quickly. "I'm just—trying to help."

He stared at me like he was peeling me apart. "Helping would've been keeping your shit together back when you had a job. Instead, you let everything fall apart, and now I'm the one covering bills."

"I didn't let it fall apart," I whispered.

"What was that?"

I stared at my plate. "You said I should quit. You said it was too much."

"I said, it was embarrassing watching you run around town pretending to be some big-time designer. You barely had any clients. Who were you kidding?"

My throat tightened. I pushed the toast away, no longer pretending.

"You gonna cry now?" he asked, standing slowly. "Jesus. Don't be so dramatic. I'm just being honest."

He passed behind me, brushing my shoulder harder than necessary. I stayed still, fingers digging into the counter's edge.

"You want honesty, right?" he said, reaching for his keys. "Or are we still doing that thing—pretending your feelings matter?"

I flinched before I could stop myself. His eyes caught the movement, and something shifted—a flicker of triumph. He liked knowing he could still get that reaction.

He opened the door halfway and paused. "Don't leave. I'm not in the mood to track your ass down today."

"I wasn't planning to."

"Good." He stepped out, then turned back smiling—but it didn't touch his eyes. "I might bring you something. Flowers, or whatever. Since you're so fucking sensitive lately."

Then he was gone. The door clicked shut, and his truck roared to life. I waited. Always waited. Just in case he came back. Sometimes he did—double back because he forgot something, or because he wanted to catch me doing something he could accuse me of later.

Five minutes. Ten. I listened for the sound of gravel under tires. Nothing.

I let out a breath I hadn't realized I'd been holding.

The quiet that followed wasn't peace. It was a hollow kind of stillness that settled in like smoke—hard to breathe through. I moved slowly through the kitchen, clearing his plate even though he hadn't used one. Just crumbs. I wiped them up anyway. I always did. It gave me something to do with my hands.

I walked into the living room and stood in the center, scanning it like a stranger. Beige walls. Beige couch. Beige throw pillows. I used to love color. My Jeep still sat outside, a memory from another life—yellow, bright, unapologetic. He called it obnoxious. Said it drew attention.

I hadn't driven it in weeks.

I sank onto the couch and pulled the blanket around my shoulders. My fingers traced the threads absentmindedly. My body ached—not from anything new, but from the constant tension. The way I always held myself too tightly. Like bracing for an earthquake that never ended.

The TV remote sat on the coffee table, untouched. I didn't turn it on. I didn't want sound. I didn't want silence either. I just sat there, somewhere in between.

My eyes drifted to the bookshelf. A row of novels I hadn't touched in months. Some still had bookmarks halfway through. I used to devour books. Now, I couldn't focus on a single page. My mind wandered too much, replayed conversations I didn't want to remember, rehearsing ones I'd never have.

The clock on the wall ticked, loud and steady. I counted the seconds, letting them wrap around me.

I should have showered. I should have eaten. I should have done laundry, gone outside, or opened a window. But I stayed where I was. The idea of moving felt heavy. I closed my eyes and leaned back, head against the cushion.

Instead, I thought about the time we drove out to Provo just to get donuts from that place I liked. He held my hand the whole way, played my favorite songs, told me I looked beautiful even in sweatpants. I remember laughing until I couldn't breathe when he tripped getting out of the truck.

But even then, there were signs. I remembered how he got pissed when I took too long to pick a donut. How he told the cashier to "hurry the hell up" because he hated waiting. I remember the way his smile faded the second we were back in the car, how he didn't talk to me the whole drive home because I said I didn't like one of his playlist songs.

It used to be so easy to ignore that stuff.

I pressed my fingertips against my temples, rubbing them in slow circles. My head throbbed with a dull ache that felt like it had lived there for weeks.

I couldn't even cry—that was the worst part. I wanted to. I felt like I should, but the tears never came. A tight, knotted thing sat in my chest, heavy and unmoving.

A door slammed outside. I jolted upright.

Just the neighbors.

I rubbed my arms, skin cold beneath the blanket. Time passed slowly. I lost track of how long I sat there—long enough for the light to shift on the walls, for shadows to stretch across the floor.

Eventually, I stood. Forced myself to walk to the bathroom. The mirror over the sink caught my face. I looked...thin . Cheeks hollowed. Skin pale, dull. My eyes—God, my eyes looked older than they should.

I turned on the faucet and splashed water on my face. It didn't help.

He'd be home soon.

I had maybe twenty more minutes of quiet. Twenty more minutes before I needed to brace myself again. Before the questions, the jabs, the moods that turned without warning.

I went back to the kitchen, opened the fridge, and pulled out a container of chicken I'd cooked two days ago. He'd said it was dry. I picked at it cold. I wasn't hungry—not really. Just needed something in my stomach. Something to keep me upright.

The clock kept ticking.

I heard the low growl of his truck before I saw it. Tires crunching over gravel. My spine stiffened. I set the container down and froze.

The front door opened. His boots landed heavy, same rhythm as always. He didn't call out. Just moved through the space like he owned the air.

And maybe he did. Maybe that was the point. Every breath I took felt borrowed. Every move calculated.

He walked into the kitchen. Glanced at me. "You make dinner?"

"No," I said.

He looked at the chicken on the counter. "What's this?"

"Leftovers."

He stared at me for a second. Then shrugged. "Fine."

I stepped aside so he could pass.

As he opened the fridge, I turned and went back to the living room, sinking into the couch with my knees pulled tight to my chest.

There were no fights that night. No blows. No shouting. Just quiet disapproval. Passive barbs—the kind that carved deeper because they didn't leave bruises you could show someone.

That was how most days were.

The pasta boiled over before I noticed. A hiss of water hit the stove top, steam curling upward, thick and sudden. I scrambled to turn the burner down, flicking it too far, then back again. The sauce was too thin. I'd stirred it too much—or not enough, I didn't know anymore. My hands moved on their own, grabbing a spoon, mixing again, trying to fix something that wouldn't be fixed. The smell of garlic clung to my skin. The kitchen light buzzed faintly overhead.

I'd tried—God, I had tried—to make it good tonight. He said he wanted something home-cooked. "Real food," he called it. Not leftovers, not whatever half-assed thing I scraped together between cleaning and staring at the floor.

I'd used the last of the Parmesan he liked. Burned my wrist pulling the bread from the oven. Set the table with actual silverware, not the mismatched forks we usually used. I'd even changed my shirt, one of the few he hadn't ruined with some offhand insult. Pale blue, soft cotton, sleeves that didn't show the fading yellow marks on my upper arms.

He walked through the door later than usual. I heard keys hit the counter, heavy and careless, then the fridge open and shut. His boots tracked dry dirt across the tile I'd mopped twice earlier.

He didn't say anything at first. Just walked past, grabbed a beer, and flopped down at the table like a man twice his age, sighing dramatically.

I turned toward him, wiping my palms on a dish towel. "It's ready."

He popped the cap; let it clink onto the table without looking. "Smells like burnt garlic."

"It's just the bread."

He took a long drink, set the bottle down hard enough to make the table tremble. "Didn't you use the timer?"

I nodded. "I just... pulled it a little late."

His eyes slid toward me, flat, unreadable. "You know I hate burnt shit."

"It's not burnt. Just a little crispy."

"Same damn thing."

My throat tightened, but I said nothing. I turned and started plating the food—sauce over noodles, a slice of bread on the side. I brought him his plate first, set it down with both hands so I didn't drop it.

He stabbed the noodles like they'd offended him.

I sat across, heart thudding faster than it should. I watched him, chew, swallow, then push the plate slightly away.

"Too salty."

I blinked. "It's the same sauce I've always made."

He picked at the bread. "No. It's off. Did you even taste it before you served it?"

"I did."

He scoffed. "Guess your standards dropped."

Something in me tightened, like a cord pulled too taut. I picked at my food, but the taste turned sour in my mouth.

"You know what," he said, leaning back, beer in hand, "you've been slipping lately. It's like you're not even trying anymore."

I looked up, my fork halfway to my mouth. "I made dinner. I cleaned. I've done every damn thing you've asked."

He raised his eyebrows, slow and deliberate. "Everything I've asked?"

My voice shook, but I didn't look away. "Yeah. What more do you want?"

His chair scraped the floor as he pushed it back and stood. His movements slow, deliberate, almost too casual. He leaned on the table with both hands and looked at me like I'd just kicked his dog. "Don't get smart with me."

"I'm not." I stood too, heart pounding. "I'm just tired."

"Of what?" His tone sharpened, slicing through the air. "Living rent-free? Eating on my dime?"

"I quit my job because you told me to."

"Because it was a goddamn mess! You were running around acting like you were something special, and you weren't. No one was gonna pay you for that fake-ass design work."

My chest burned. I hadn't brought it up—not in months—it festered in him anyway, like everything else he couldn't control. I took a slow step back, voice quiet. "Don't talk to me like that."

His jaw flexed. "Or what?"

I held his stare. That was a mistake.

His hand moved faster than my brain could process. It crashed against my cheek; the sound snapped the air open. My head jerked sideways. I stumbled, grasping for the counter to stay upright. The sting bloomed instantly—hot, sharp, radiating from the bone out. My ear rang.

I didn't speak. My thoughts scattered like loose nails on a floor. I stared at the tile beneath my bare feet. One corner was chipped. I'd been meaning to fix it.

"Don't ever raise your voice at me again," he said, low, each word measured. "Don't act like you're owed anything."

The room went so still, I thought the walls might cave in from the pressure. My body buzzed, cold and too hot at once. I couldn't move. Couldn't think.

He walked past me like he hadn't just hit me. Like it was nothing. Like it wasn't the first time. Like maybe he'd done it a thousand times in his head already.

The bedroom door slammed shut behind him.

My breath came shallow, ragged. I touched my cheek. It burned beneath my fingers, already starting to throb. I looked at my hand. No blood. Just shaking.

I walked slowly to the sink and turned on the cold tap. Pressed a dish towel under it, then brought it to my face. The cold shocked me. I held it there, pressing harder than I needed to. I stared at my reflection in the dark window over the sink, barely making out the blur of myself.

The woman staring back didn't look like me. Not the girl who used to dance barefoot in the grass. Not the one who sang too loud in her Jeep with the top off, hair tangled in the wind. She was gone—stripped down to something thin and breakable.

I sank to the floor. Pulled my knees up. Rested my forehead against them. My ribs ached from holding everything in.

He'd never hit me before.

Yelled, yes. Grabbed my arm too hard. Thrown things across the room. But this was different. This crossed some invisible line I hadn't let myself believe existed.

The tears didn't come right away. My eyes just burned.

I sat there until the floor chilled through my legs. I lost track of time.

He didn't come back out. Didn't say a word.

The silence wasn't peace. It was strategy. He wanted me to stew in it. To second-guess myself. To replay what I said. To wonder if I pushed him too far.

Eventually, I stood. Legs stiff, hands still trembling. I cleaned up the dishes like a goddamn robot. Washed the uneaten food down the drain. Scrubbed the counter. Folded the dish towel. All the while, my face throbbed.

The bathroom mirror showed the start of a bruise—dark under the skin. I pulled out my makeup bag, dabbed concealer over it. The color didn't match. I pressed harder. My hands shook.

I washed them three times, scrubbing until the skin reddened.

By the time I crawled into bed, he was already asleep—or pretending to be. His back to me. Breathing deep.

I lay stiff on my side, afraid to move, afraid not to. The room felt too quiet. I stared at the ceiling and counted seconds, then minutes, until my eyes blurred.

I didn't sleep. I didn't cry. I just waited. For what, I wasn't sure. But something cracked wide open inside me, and I knew—deep down—that nothing would ever go back to what it was. Not because I didn't want it to, but because some things, once broken, stopped pretending to be whole.

The Sound of Silence

The morning began the same way most of them did now—with silence sharp enough to split bone. He left the bedroom without a word, not even a glance, letting the door swing shut behind him hard enough to rattle the frame. I'd been awake already, curled on the far edge of the mattress, eyes fixed on the uneven seam in the drywall, body stiff beneath the covers. I waited until the sound of his boots reached the kitchen before I sat up, every movement slow, careful, deliberate.

I walked barefoot, toes curling against the cold tile. The air smelled like stale sweat and burnt coffee grounds—the kind that sat on the burner too long. He always made it too strong, scooping more grounds in out of habit or spite, I couldn't tell.

I found him hunched over his phone at the table, the same chair he always sat in, elbows planted, thumb swiping. No greeting. Not even a glance as I stepped around him toward the coffee pot. The lid was crooked. Grounds floated on top like scum in a muddy pond. I poured a cup anyway, hands steady, even though my insides curled tighter with each second, he refused to acknowledge me.

He tapped the screen harder than necessary. A sigh tore from his chest, long and exaggerated. His knee bounced beneath the table.

I kept my voice soft, testing the air. "Do you want breakfast?"

Nothing.

My spine tensed. I tried again. "I was going to make eggs. Or—there's still oatmeal."

He stood suddenly, the chair scraping back. Not a word. He walked to the fridge, yanked the door open so hard the shelves rattled and grabbed a beer. Nine in the goddamn morning and he was drinking. The bottle hissed as he cracked it open. He never looked at me once.

He moved to the sink, sipping slowly as if I didn't exist two feet away.

I turned to the counter and opened the drawer with the spatulas. Closed it. Opened it again, slower this time. My hands hovered. I didn't know whether to cook or disappear.

He finally muttered something under his breath, too quiet for me to make out.

"What?"

He slammed the bottle down. "Jesus, are you deaf now too?"

My breath caught, then steadied. "I didn't hear you."

"I said—don't make anything. I don't want your half-assed cooking."

The sting didn't come from the words. Not anymore. It was his tone, flat, disgusted, like I was some filthy thing he'd found beneath his boot.

"Okay," I whispered.

He grabbed his keys and wallet from the counter. His eyes met mine for the first time that morning—cold and unreadable. He didn't say goodbye. Just turned and slammed the door on his way out.

I didn't move for a long time. Just stood there, gripping the edge of the counter, staring at the bottle he'd left by the sink. Condensation slid down the glass, pooling beneath it.

Eventually, I sat at the table. My coffee had gone cold. I didn't care.

I didn't cry; I never did during the day anymore. My body saved that for when the lights went out and the house was quiet. The bruises were easier to hide than the tremble in my voice when I forgot to stay small.

The rest of the morning dragged. I wiped down the already clean counters, straightened the magazines on the coffee table he never touched, folded a load of laundry wasn't mine. I didn't even realize I was doing it until I caught myself smoothing the crease in his favorite hoodie.

By noon, I'd swept the porch, watered the dusty plant by the front door, and reorganized the spice cabinet. Every few minutes, I paused to listen for his truck in the driveway. Nothing.

It was a weird kind of peace, the hours when he was gone. A fragile quiet buzzed under my skin like static. I couldn't relax, not really, but I could breathe without flinching.

When the afternoon sun began cutting through the front window, I opened it a crack. Just a little fresh air. Just enough to catch the scent of dry earth and faint smoke from someone burning wood down the road.

I made a sandwich I didn't want and ate it standing up. My appetite was something I ignored now. Some days I forgot food entirely. Other days I stuffed myself just to feel something besides fear.

When I heard the truck pull up around five, I froze. Bread halfway to the trash. My heart did this little jolt—more reflex than emotion. I wiped my hands, closed the trash can, checked my reflection in the microwave door. No food on my shirt. No dishes left out. Nothing out of place.

The door opened slowly this time. He walked in without looking at me. No greeting. Just stomped across the room, dropped his keys in the bowl on the table, and sank into the recliner, like he'd had a rough day working for a cause no one appreciated.

I stood by the fridge, pretending to read a note stuck there from months ago.

"Where's the mail?" he asked.

"I—there wasn't any."

His jaw twitched. "You sure?"

"Yes. I checked earlier."

He didn't respond. Just stared at the TV, remote in hand, clicking through channels, not settling on anything.

"Do you want dinner later?"

His thumb paused. "You asking because you actually want to do something right or just filling the silence?"

I bit my tongue. "I just thought you might be hungry."

He laughed. It was dry, mean. "You're always thinking, aren't you?"

I didn't answer. I couldn't win either way.

"Make something decent. None of that dry chicken shit."

"Okay."

"And don't overcook the pasta this time."

My pulse beat faster. "Alright."

He stood and stretched like a man twice his age. "I'm going to shower. That thing better be ready when I get out."

"Got it."

He walked past me, his shoulder grazing my arm-—not hard, but enough. Enough to remind me I was in his way.

I moved quickly. Started the water boiling, pulled the pasta from the pantry, defrosted some meat. My hands knew the rhythm by now. It was almost meditative—until the panic kicked in. What if it's too salty? What if it's underdone? What if he smells something he doesn't like and flips out?

The shower cut off as I was straining the noodles—I rushed to finish. The plates were out, food was hot, everything was set the way he liked. I even grabbed a second beer from the fridge.

He walked back into the kitchen, hair damp, white shirt clinging to his back. He sniffed the air—didn't say anything. Just sat.

I brought his plate. He didn't thank me. He took one bite, then another, chewing slowly.

"It's fine," he said finally.

Relief loosened something in my shoulders.

"Don't just stand there," he said, mouth full. "Sit."

I obeyed, picking at the food on my plate. It tasted bland. Or maybe it was just me.

He kept eating, paused once to reach for the beer. "See? Not that hard when you actually give a shit."

I nodded.

We ate in near silence. He turned the TV on midway through. Sound filled the space, numbing it.

After dinner, I cleaned up while he lounged. He didn't offer to help—he never did.

By nine, he was already halfway through a third beer, sprawled out on the couch like a king.

"You gonna sit with me, or hover all night?"

I wiped my hands on a towel and moved to the edge of the couch. I sat, legs tucked under me, careful not to touch him.

He looked over. "What's with you lately?"

"What do you mean?"

"You've been weird. Quiet."

"I didn't want to upset you."

His laugh was cold. "You're always walking around like I'm some kind of monster."

I said nothing.

"You think I like acting like this?" he asked, shifting closer. "You think I enjoy losing my temper?"

"I don't know."

He stared at me, eyes narrowed. "You push. You always push. Then you act surprised when I react."

My chest tightened. "I'm not trying to push."

He leaned in. "Then stop looking at me like I'm gonna hit you."

I flinched.

"Goddamn it," he said, standing abruptly. "You make me feel like a fucking psycho."

He stormed off to the bedroom, slamming the door behind him.

I sat frozen on the couch, nails digging into the fabric of my jeans. My face burned even though he hadn't touched me.

It was never about what he did, it was about how he made me feel like I was the problem. Like I was the one unraveling this whole mess.

The silence afterward was louder than anything he had said. I stared at the dark TV screen. My reflection stared back, blurry and pale.

By noon I'd already wiped down the baseboards with vinegar and water. Every single one. Crawling along the hallway, like a ghost in my own damn house, sponge in one hand, old towel in the other. The tile grout was next. Then I vacuumed the living room—even though I'd done it two days ago. Pulled out the couch cushions, beat them out back, put them back just right. Checked them from all angles. No crumbs. No lint. Nothing he could comment on—nothing he could use.

The silence pressed harder than usual. It had that thick, heavy drag to it—like walking through mud. I turned on the old radio we kept in the corner of the kitchen and set it to static, before I flipped it off again. Too loud. I didn't want him coming home, hearing it and deciding it meant something. He'd find a way to make it wrong. He always did.

The fridge hummed behind me as I stood there, clutching a damp rag and staring at the clean floor like it held a map out of all this. The mop bucket sat beside me, water gone lukewarm, rag already stiffening around the edges. The clock above the stove ticked, as if it was mocking me. Three hours until he got home. Maybe four, if he went to the bar.

I cracked the window above the sink open, just enough to let in air, not enough to let in sound. Sat at the table and checked my phone—no messages, no calls. Just one old email from a past client that I'd never answered. I'd meant to. Back then. Before everything crumbled.

I held the phone in both hands and scrolled through old texts like they were artifacts. My sister's name showed up near the top. Lemon. A nickname, her given name was Lennon. My own being, Honey, Austin hated it and never used it. I hadn't called her in months. Not since he accused me of "telling lies about him" when she asked too many questions. He said, I made had him look like a bad guy. Said I needed to learn some loyalty. He said it as a warning, not a plea.

I locked the phone and pressed it against my thigh until it hurt.

The meat was thawing in the fridge, the veggies chopped, everything prepped in their little bowls like I was hosting a dinner party for someone who wouldn't even look at me. I pulled the casserole dish from the cupboard and greased it with slow, even strokes. Every motion had become quiet ceremony. I did it all the way he liked—chicken layered first, cream sauce on top, cheese last. I didn't rush it. Didn't skip a step. Not because I wanted him to be pleased, but because I didn't want him to have a reason.

When I slid it into the oven, I realized my hands were shaking. Just a slight tremble, but enough I had to steady them on the counter top. The heat of the oven prickled against my skin, too warm for the room, and I leaned away from it.

I sat back down, folded the rag neatly beside me. Checked my phone again—still nothing.

I began to wonder what today's infraction had been. Maybe I used too much hot water last night. Maybe I was too quiet during dinner. Maybe he heard something in my voice that he didn't like—it didn't matter. There was no rulebook, no system. No way to track the shifting moods or draw a clean line between cause and punishment.

The back door creaked when the wind pushed against it. I stood fast, heart jumping. Just the wind. Just the shitty old latch we never replaced. I still went and checked the lock anyway. Then I checked the front door, then the windows. The routine made no sense, but it gave me something to do.

I walked into the bedroom and straightened the already made bed. Ran my hand over the comforter smoothing out the folds. Fixed the angle of the lamp. Fluffed the pillow he liked. Then I checked the timer on the oven, and paced the hallway.

The sound of gravel under tires made me freeze. Not a full stop—just that slow, stiff pause like prey in the woods when a twig snaps nearby. I peeked through the curtain. His truck was there. Five o'clock sharp. Earlier than I expected. My breath tightened.

I checked the oven again. Dinner still had twenty minutes left. That wouldn't go over well.

I stood by the sink, trying to look busy. The door opened, his keys hit the counter with a thud. He didn't say anything.

He didn't look at me.

He walked straight into the living room, where he dropped onto the couch. Remote in hand. TV on. Volume up.

I walked toward the living room, but stopped in the doorway. "Hey. Dinner's in the oven. It needs a little more time."

He didn't glance my way.

I swallowed. "Should be good tonight."

He turned the volume up.

I stood there another few seconds before walking back to the kitchen. My throat burned, but I shoved it down and set the table. His favorite plate, silverware to the left, napkin folded just right. Beer from the fridge, cracked and ready.

By the time I pulled the dish from the oven, he still hadn't moved. I served his plate and brought it to him, setting it down on the coffee table, since he hadn't come to the kitchen.

He glanced down. "What is it?"

"Chicken bake. The one with the cream sauce."

He picked up the fork like it offended him before he stabbed at the food. He took a bite and chewed it. No reaction.

I waited, stomach clenched with anxiety.

He swallowed before he muttered, "It's fine."

I nodded and backed away, walking into the kitchen where I ate my plate cold. Every bite stuck in my throat, but I forced it down. I didn't want to hear him ask why I wasn't eating. Didn't want to hear that I was "starving myself for attention again."

When I cleaned up his plate, he didn't say thank you. Just handed it over like I was a waitress without a name. I washed it silently, hands moving slow through the water.

Later, I sat across the room while he watched something stupid and loud on the TV. My phone stayed tucked in the pocket of my hoodie, screen untouched. I didn't dare scroll. Didn't want him thinking I was talking to anyone. Last time, he'd accused me of sneaking around behind his back. I still had the scar on my thigh from the bottle he broke during that argument. It was not thrown at me, he'd said. But thrown, because of me.

At ten, he stood and stretched. "Going to bed."

"Okay," I said, voice barely above a whisper.

He glanced at me, eyes narrowed. "What?"

"I said, okay."

He watched me another beat, trying to read something on my face. Then he turned and walked to the bedroom.

I stayed in the living room, lights low, staring at a blank screen long after the TV went off. My ears still rang from the volume. My neck ached from how long I had sat still.

Eventually, I curled up on the couch, pulling the blanket over my shoulders, and stared at the darkened corner by the door. The quiet had weight. Not peace. Not calm. Just pressure. It stretched across the floor and wrapped itself around me.

I didn't cry. Not yet. Not until I was sure he wouldn't come back out to find me, curled up like something useless. Then maybe, if the dark was thick enough and the house still enough, I'd let myself fall apart quietly—without anyone to hear it.

Honey, I'm Home

His truck rumbled up the drive just before six. The low growl of the engine sent a jolt of panic through my ribs. I stood in the kitchen, hands resting on the edge of the counter, staring at the browned crust of the baked potatoes and the roasted vegetables laid out in perfect symmetry. The chicken sat under a foil tent, resting as if being prepared for inspection. I'd timed everything so nothing would dry out, nothing would go cold. Not again.

The door opened slower than usual—no slam—just the creeping quiet that always made me more nervous. His boots hit the tile one step at a time, like he wanted to be sure I heard every inch of his entrance. He passed through the kitchen without looking at me, dropped his keys into the ceramic bowl beside the fridge, then walked to the bathroom and turned on the faucet. The water ran too long for hand washing—probably splashing his face. Or staring at it.

I adjusted the plates again. Centered them. Checked the butter for the third time, twisted the salt grinder just to give my fingers something to do.

He came back into the kitchen, still not saying anything. His shirt was damp at the collar and he smelled faintly of sawdust and sweat and stale fast-food grease. The scent clung to him like it had soaked into his skin.

"Dinner's ready," I offered, too soft. I cleared my throat. "You want a beer?"

He opened the fridge without answering, grabbed one himself, popped the cap with the edge of the counter, like I wasn't standing right there. He took a long swig, leaned against the wall, and scanned the table like he was waiting for something to offend him.

"This what you made?" His voice had that tone again—flat, bored, like he already hated it.

"Yeah. I thought I'd try the new seasoning blend on the chick—"

"You thought?" He snorted, shaking his head. "That's rich."

I kept my face neutral and stepped back to the counter. "It's just garlic, paprika... it's nothing weird."

He walked to the table, dropped into the chair with a grunt, and looked down at the plate I'd set for him. "What's with the presentation? You trying to impress somebody?"

My stomach flipped, but I forced a laugh. "I was just… trying to make it nice."

"Looks like you tried to copy some Pinterest shit but gave up halfway through." He shoved the vegetables around with his fork, then took a bite of chicken. Chewing with exaggerated slowness. "Dry," he said with his mouth full.

"I followed the recipe exactly."

"Maybe the recipe wasn't the problem." He stabbed another piece, shoveled it in. "You ever think it's just you?"

I looked down at my plate, appetite gone, hands clenched in my lap. "I'll do something different next time."

He snorted again and took another drink. "Next time, maybe try not fucking it up."

My cheeks burned. I wasn't sure if it was anger or shame anymore. Probably both. I picked at a piece of broccoli, brought it to my mouth, but it tasted like metal. I chewed slowly, forcing it down.

He wiped his mouth on the back of his hand, before gesturing vaguely toward me. "What's with the shirt?"

I looked down. I wore a faded soft tee I'd had for years. Blue, loose-fitting. Comfortable. I hadn't worn anything revealing. I never did anymore. "What about it?"

"Looks sloppy." His eyes narrowed. "You gonna stay looking like that all day, or…?"

I shook my head, voice low. "I was home all day. I cleaned, cooked, I didn't think—"

"Yeah, that's the issue right there." He leaned back, beer in hand, the corner of his mouth curling. "You don't think."

I laughed again, too quick, brittle. "Guess I walked into that one, huh?"

His grin widened like he'd just won something. "Finally catching on."

The room felt smaller. My skin felt too tight. I pressed my tongue, hard, against the roof of my mouth just to keep quiet. He went back to eating, scooping up another bite without looking up. The sound of his fork scraping the plate drilled into my ears. I forced another bite of my own food, but it just sat there in my mouth, tasteless and dry.

He reached for the napkin, dabbed at his chin, then tossed it beside the plate. "This better not give me heartburn."

"It's not spicy."

"Yeah, well. Sometimes even your bland shit makes my stomach turn."

I nodded. The jab didn't even sting the way it used to—just landed like another dull thud.

He looked up finally, eyes locking on mine like he was studying something under glass. "Why're you so damn quiet tonight?"

"I didn't think you wanted to talk."

"Don't act like I'm the one sulking."

"I'm not."

"Could've fooled me." He leaned forward, elbows on the table. "You walking around here all mopey, staring at your phone like someone died."

"I wasn't—"

He cut me off with a laugh. "Right. I forgot, you've got nobody to talk to."

My throat closed as I reached for my water, taking a sip to give myself something to do. Something to keep the burn from my eyes.

"You should be grateful," he added. "I come home, I eat your food, I don't even complain that much."

I nodded again, pressing the glass harder into the table than I meant to.

He cocked his head. "You think you'd last a week on your own?"

"I don't know."

"You don't know?" His voice dropped, mockingly soft. "You think you could pay rent? Buy groceries? Fix your precious little Jeep when it shits out again?"

My hands tightened around the glass, but I didn't answer.

He kept going. "You're not some strong independent woman, alright? I saved you from that pathetic little business, and your pathetic little life."

"I never asked you to—"

He slammed his fist against the table. Not hard enough to knock anything over. Just enough to shut me up.

The sound snapped through my body like electricity. My heart kicked, jaw clamped shut.

"Don't talk back to me."

I nodded quickly, chest squeezing.

He stood, taking his plate and the empty beer bottle with him. "I'm gonna shower. Better not leave this mess here when I get out."

"Okay."

He walked off, muttering something under his breath I couldn't make out. The bathroom door clicked shut a second later, and the sound of the water starting up followed like clockwork.

I sat staring at the wood grain of the table. My eyes had gone dry; I couldn't even blink without them stinging. The food on my plate was cold, congealed into something inedible. I hadn't even noticed I was gripping my fork so tight until my fingers were numb.

I stood slowly, legs stiff, knees aching from how tense they'd been. I gathered the plates. His first, then mine. I carried them to the sink and turned on the water. Let it run too long before I reached for the soap.

The steam hit my face—the heat helped. Not much, but enough. Enough to keep me from unraveling where he might hear.

The water from the faucet was too hot, but I didn't turn it down. It burned across my knuckles as I scrubbed the dishes with the old green sponge, the one that always left little threads behind no matter how many times I rinsed it. The plates were clean, but I kept scrubbing, trying to erase something that wasn't on the surface. Steam fogged the window above the sink. My skin was damp with it, hair beginning to curl at my temples.

The bathroom door creaked open behind me. I didn't look. I could hear him moving—bare feet against the tile, a sharp sigh, the scrape of a chair leg. The fridge opened, then closed. The bottle cap hit the counter, then the glug of beer poured into one of the heavy glass cups we never used for guests, because there were never guests.

I reached for his plate, the last one left on the drying rack, and froze. His glass. I hadn't rinsed it before putting it in the rack. The remnants of whatever he drank before dinner were still clinging to the sides—some weird mix of Gatorade and energy powder he liked after work.

He stepped up behind me before I could grab it. His breath hit the back of my neck. My spine stiffened. His hand slid around my wrist, not gently, and yanked it up like I was a misbehaving child.

"What the fuck is this?"

My heart jumped. "I forgot. I'm sorry. I thought I rinsed it—"

"You thought?" His fingers tightened. "You're not paid to think, remember?"

Pain shot up my arm, fast and hot. I tried to twist away, but he just gripped harder. The edge of the counter pressed into my hip. I bit my lip to keep from reacting.

"I'll fix it," I whispered.

He let go suddenly, and I stumbled a little before I caught myself on the edge of the sink.

"Fix it then," he said, and turned away like the entire exchange hadn't just happened.

I turned back to the sink and grabbed the cup, rinsed it out, washed it again even though my hand throbbed now. My wrist had already begun to swell, the skin around it turning a blotchy red. I held it under the cold water when he wasn't looking. Not for long. Just enough to take the sting down a notch.

He was sitting on the couch by the time I finished. Legs sprawled out, one arm slung across the back, beer in hand like a king after war. He was watching some trash show—loud, obnoxious, with people yelling over each other about nothing.

I dried my hands, set the towel down, and walked past him, hoping he wouldn't reach for me again. I didn't trust my own reactions anymore. Didn't know what I'd say if I let myself speak.

"Come here," he said, not taking his eyes off the screen.

"I need to—"

"Now."

I turned and stepped closer, standing in front of him like he was a cop pulling me over.

He reached out, tugging at the hem of my shirt. "You always act like I'm gonna beat you to death. You know how fucked up that is?"

I opened my mouth, but nothing came out. He pulled me forward by the fabric, his fingers brushed my bruised wrist. I flinched without meaning to.

He noticed. Smiled a little.

"Don't be dramatic." Then he leaned in and kissed me—wet, too firm, breath thick with beer and mouthwash.

My body didn't move. Didn't lean into it. Didn't pull away. Just stayed.

He patted my hip like I was a dog and leaned back again.

"Go get ready for bed," he said, like it was a normal night, like we were done with whatever just happened.

I walked back to the bedroom, shutting the door softly behind me. The overhead light flickered once before staying on. I sat on the edge of the bed and looked down at my wrist. The bruise was already forming, purpling near the bone. I touched it gently, winced. It felt like someone had dropped a rock on it.

I changed into a t-shirt—an old one, over-sized and soft. The cotton rubbed against the new bruise and I pulled the sleeve down to cover it. Not because he cared if it showed. Because I didn't want to see it.

He came in ten minutes later, shirtless, laughing at something that happened on the TV. Still riding whatever high that show gave him. He pulled the blankets back, dropped into bed with a grunt, and reached for me automatically, like he expected me to slide in beside him and press into his side.

I hesitated.

"What?" he asked, voice half-tired, half-annoyed.

"Nothing."

"Don't pull that mood shit."

"I'm not."

"Then lay down."

I climbed beneath the covers, keeping my body close to the edge of the mattress. I curled away, careful not to let my wrist brush against anything. He rolled over and faced the wall, and just like that, the night turned off.

His breathing slowed. Became steady. Became even. Maybe fake.

I stared at the ceiling. The shadows there looked like cracks. The kind that spiderweb across old glass right before it breaks.

I used to think love meant safety. Warm hands. Soft laughter. I used to think it meant being held at night, not bruised. I used to think love looked like sunflowers and road trips and playlists made for long drives. Not being told to rinse a glass better. Not being yanked around like I was part of the furniture.

He used to call me Sunshine—said I lit up rooms. Said I made him better. That was back when he smiled with his eyes. Back when he brushed my hair behind my ear instead of tugging on it when I annoyed him.

My eyes stayed wide open, focused on the small rip in the corner of the bedsheet. I should've stitched weeks ago. He said I let the house go. Maybe he was right.

I rolled slightly, careful not to shift the mattress too much. My bruised wrist rested on my stomach, throbbing with each pulse.

Was love supposed to feel this confusing?

I turned toward the nightstand and watched the digital clock blink. Red numbers ticked past midnight. My chest felt hollow. The kind of hollow that echoed if I dared to speak into it. So, I just didn't.

I just stayed there, curled on the far side of the bed, tracing the outline of the bruise with my mind, wondering if I'd be able to cover it tomorrow. Wondering if he'd kiss me again in the morning, like none of this mattered. Like I was still his Sunshine.

My eyes burned, but I didn't cry. I just listened to the sound of his breathing. I stayed quiet. I stayed small. I stayed where he left me.

Coffee and Confessions

I STOOD BY THE sink, holding the grocery list like it was some kind of passport. The paper trembled slightly in my hand, even though the kitchen was warm. I'd written out everything in neat rows, categorized just the way he liked—produce, meat, dry goods, household. There was nothing indulgent on the list, nothing unnecessary. No fresh flowers. No chocolate. No magazines, or candles, or nail polish. Just things that could be eaten, used, counted.

He was sitting on the couch with one boot still on, the other tossed somewhere by the door. The TV was playing a commercial for some truck dealership, volume up too high. He had a beer in his hand and the look he got when he was barely holding onto the mood he wanted me to believe was calm. His shoulders were loose, but his jaw wasn't.

"I'm heading out."

He didn't answer right away. Just adjusted himself on the cushion and stared at the screen. When I reached for the keys off the hook, he finally said, "Don't take forever."

"I won't."

"Get the right rice this time. None of that off-brand shit."

"Got it."

"And if they don't have those turkey burgers I like, don't guess. Text me."

"I will."

He turned the volume up again.

I slid on my shoes by the door, fingers moving fast over the laces. The bruising on my wrist was yellowing around the edges, fading just enough I could push up my sleeves again, if I was careful. I pulled on a jacket anyway, the soft denim kind with the worn elbows and the pocket I'd sewn up after it split last fall. The keys jingled in my hand, louder than they needed to be.

When I stepped outside, the air was sharp with the leftover chill of spring refusing to fully give way to summer. My breath came tight at first, then looser as I got to the Jeep. I climbed in, shut the door gently, and rested my hands on the wheel for a second.

He hadn't asked to come. That was something. He usually didn't trust me to do anything alone, but lately, he seemed too tired to micromanage every breath I took. Or maybe he thought the fear had settled enough inside me that I'd police myself now.

The drive to the store was automatic. Right on Main. Past the same old gas station with the broken ice machine. Through the four-way stop that no one in town knew how to use properly. My fingers tightened around the steering wheel as I approached the turn for the grocery lot. I slowed. Signaled. Then kept driving.

My heart kicked once, hard.

The turnoff to Salt City Brews was five blocks farther.

I didn't even know what I was doing until the café's brown brick storefront came into view. The green awning had a small tear in one corner, flapping in the wind like it was waving me in. I turned the wheel and pulled into the lot, parked in the back near the dumpster, just in case someone he knew saw me. Just in case he checked. Just in case.

The Jeep's engine ticked as it cooled. I sat there, staring at the building. My hands rested in my lap. No one came yelling. No one came to stop me. The silence inside the car was steady. I looked down at the list on the passenger seat. The first line said "milk." The last said "toilet paper." Not a single thing on it was for me.

I left the list where it was.

The café door gave a familiar squeak as I pushed it open. Warm air rushed over me, carrying the smell of espresso, cinnamon, and baked things I used to let myself enjoy. The place hadn't changed. The same chalkboard menus, the same mismatched mugs on the shelf above the pastry case, the same hum of conversation and clatter of cups. For a second, I just stood there, blinking against the soft light, unsure if I really belonged here.

"Hey there." The girl behind the counter smiled. She had a tiny hoop in her nose and dark curls piled into a messy bun. "What can I get you?"

I stepped forward, brushing a hand over the seam of my jacket. "A latte. Vanilla. And—uh—one of those cranberry scones."

She nodded and rang it up. "For here or to go?"

I hesitated. "To stay."

I paid cash, crumpled bills from the side pocket of my wallet that he never checked. She handed me a tiny number flag on a stick and waved me toward the open tables.

I picked one in the corner, near the front window. It was too bright, too exposed, but it felt like the safest place to sit. I watched her prep the drink behind the counter, her movements fluid and practiced. The espresso machine hissed, steam clouding up behind her.

A man at the next table typed on a laptop. A couple by the window shared a muffin. Two teenagers stood by the register, arguing over what to order. No one looked at me. No one cared that I didn't belong to anyone here. That I hadn't asked for permission.

When the girl brought over the drink and scone, I thanked her. She smiled again and left.

I wrapped my hands around the mug, letting the heat soak into my skin. The scent was warm and sweet. I took a small sip, letting the foam hit my tongue first. The taste was almost too much—rich and soft and a little too good for someone like me. It lodged in my throat before sliding down.

The scone was flaky; sugar dusted on top. I tore a piece off and placed it in my mouth slowly, letting it sit there like I was afraid to bite into it. I chewed. Swallowed. Another sip. The noise around me dulled. The hum of voices, the clink of spoons, the occasional hiss of the espresso machine. It all pressed together into something that didn't ask anything of me.

I didn't check my phone.

I didn't look at the clock.

I just sat, knees pressed together under the table, one hand around the mug, the other resting in my lap. My wrist still ached, but I'd gotten used to ignoring it.

Someone laughed near the counter. A deep laugh—familiar and sharp like boots hitting dry gravel. I turned my head slightly, but didn't see who it belonged to.

I took another bite of the scone, slower this time. I felt like I was doing something wrong, like any second someone might come up behind me and yank me out of the chair to drag me back where I was supposed to be. Where the fridge was stocked, and the dinner was hot, and glasses were rinsed without question.

I pulled the mug closer, pressed fingertips white against the ceramic.

The front door squeaked again. The cold followed, slipping under the tables and past my feet.

Someone new walked in. I didn't look. Didn't want to risk it. Just took another sip and stared out the window at the rusted bike rack and the cracked sidewalk and the old pine tree across the street with the yellowing needles.

Then I heard it.

A name I hadn't heard in years. Not spoken like that.

"Honey?"

The sound of it cut through the café noise like it had teeth. I froze, mug halfway to my lips. The hand holding the scone dropped slightly. My eyes didn't blink.

That voice.

My heart stuttered once, then surged. I didn't move. I didn't breathe.

Honey.

Olivia Reed stood just inside the doorway, her red hair pulled back in a loose braid that had half unraveled. She wore a worn flannel over a plain white tee, jeans faded at the knees, and boots dusted with dried mud like she'd just come off a horse. She looked like Grantsville—raw, honest, unpolished in a way that made my throat close.

Her eyes caught mine, and everything stopped.

"Holy shit," she said, already moving toward me. "I thought that was you."

I stood without meaning to. My knees locked, then gave a little. Her arms wrapped around me before I could say anything, before I could decide if I was ready. She held on tight, her hand pressing against the back of my jacket. I hadn't been hugged like that in a long time. Not gently. Not with no strings attached.

I didn't even realize I was crying, until I felt the wetness on her shoulder.

She pulled back, hands on my arms, her face soft and unsure, like she didn't know if she'd gone too far. "You okay?"

I nodded, shook my head, then laughed through the mess of tears. "No idea."

Olivia's eyes swept over me, careful and quick. "You look, tired," she said, like it was a polite way of saying what she was really thinking. "Sit. Let me sit with you."

We both dropped into seats, the little round café table between us. My scone sat half-eaten, forgotten. The latte had gone lukewarm. I wiped beneath my eyes with the sleeve of my jacket, feeling embarrassed even though I couldn't stop.

"You want something?" I asked, voice raspy.

She waved me off. "I came in for coffee, but now I'm staying for you."

I looked down at my hands. The bruising on my wrist peeked out from under the cuff of my jacket. I tugged the sleeve down without thinking, but Olivia's eyes caught the movement.

She didn't say anything. Just leaned back in the chair, watching me the way she used to in high school when I got quiet after my dad yelled too much.

"How long's it been?" she asked.

"Since... we talked?"

She nodded.

"Too long."

She tilted her head. "Yeah. I tried texting you last year. Thought maybe you changed your number."

"I didn't." I cleared my throat. "I just didn't answer."

She nodded again, slower this time. "Okay. You don't have to explain. I figured something was going on."

My mouth opened. Closed again. The truth pushed at my ribs, sharp and aching. I looked at her face—freckles, small scar on her jaw from when she fell off the fence post at my family's ranch. She still looked like the version of home I hadn't been allowed to think about, in a long time.

"I didn't mean to disappear."

"I know."

"It just... got complicated."

She waited. No pressure. Just sitting there, letting me have space to decide if I'd say it or not.

"I'm not okay," I said finally, quiet like I was confessing to something shameful. "It's been bad."

Her lips parted, but she didn't interrupt. Her hands rested on the edge of the table, still and open.

"I don't even know where to start."

"You don't have to get it all out at once."

I stared out the window for a second, watching a man walk his dog across the street. The leash slack, the dog tugging gently toward a patch of grass. Normal things. Simple things.

"I thought, I loved him," I said. "I did. I thought... I thought we had this thing. Like, it started out so good. He used to drive us to Provo for donuts. He played guitar sometimes, really shitty, but it made me laugh. He called me, Sunshine."

Olivia's face didn't shift, but I felt her attention sharpen.

"But then, he started getting annoyed when I talked too much. Said I was always 'doing the most.' Started telling me to quiet down in front of his friends. Little things. And then, I let go of mine. One by one. It didn't feel like a big deal when it was happening."

Her brows pulled together slightly. "You mean like friends?"

"And family," I said. "I stopped answering my sister's calls. He said she was nosy. Said she didn't respect boundaries."

"That doesn't sound like your sister."

"She wasn't the problem." I swallowed hard. "But I believed him, for a while. Or I wanted to. Because if it was my fault, then I could fix it, right?"

Olivia leaned forward slightly. "What did he do?"

I looked down at my lap. My fingers twisted the edge of the paper napkin. "The first time he hit me, it didn't feel real. It was over something small. I didn't rinse out his glass. That was it. And then—bam—he grabbed my wrist so hard I couldn't move for a day. He kissed me right after. Said, I was making him crazy."

Her eyes went dark, but she didn't speak.

"He buys me flowers sometimes. He acts like I'm his again, for a day. Then it's back to the cold shoulder. Or worse." I glanced up at her. "And I keep trying to be better, thinking if

I just do everything right, he won't snap again. But I mess up anyway. I always mess up."

"You're not the problem," Olivia said, voice low and steady.

"I don't even know who I am anymore." My voice cracked. "I used to like yellow. I haven't worn it in years because he says it makes me look washed out."

She looked like she wanted to reach across the table and grab my hands, but didn't.

"He makes me feel like I'm lucky he stuck around. Like no one else would put up with me. And sometimes, I believe it."

"You're not hard to love."

I stared at the chipped edge of the mug.

"And you're not crazy," she added.

"I used to think, love was supposed to feel like coming home," I said, my voice barely above a whisper. "Now it feels like a test I keep failing."

She took a slow breath, the kind that grounds a person before saying something real. "It's not supposed to hurt. Not like that."

I blinked fast. The burn behind my eyes crept back in.

"I didn't think I'd run into anyone today," I said.

"Well, you did." Her smile was soft now. "And I'm glad. Because I've missed you, Honey."

I wiped under my eyes again. "I shouldn't even be here. I told him I was going to the store."

"Then let's pretend this is just a different aisle."

That made me laugh, shaky and small, but real.

She looked around the café, then back at me. "Do you want to come out to the ranch sometime? No pressure. Just you, some horses, and some open space."

"I don't know if I can."

"You don't have to know yet. Just think about it."

I nodded, holding the mug tighter. "Okay."

The door squeaked again. I glanced toward it, heart jumping out of habit, but it was just a delivery guy with a crate of beans. Olivia didn't flinch. She leaned back, watching me carefully like she was trying not to spook something scared.

"Does he know you're here?"

"No."

"Does he track your phone?"

"I don't think so. Not yet."

She paused. "If you ever need to leave—"

"I don't know how," I said, cutting her off. "I don't know where I'd even start."

"You just started."

I looked at her, and something unspooled in my chest. Not all of it. Not even most of it. But enough of it.

She smiled again, and didn't ask for anything. Didn't demand I explain myself more than I already had.

The café noise faded into background again. The hiss of milk steaming. The clink of a spoon hitting ceramic. Laughter from the back corner. A familiar place full of strangers and yet—this table, this friend, this moment—felt more like home than anything I'd had in years.

I didn't know what came next. I didn't know if I'd be brave enough to leave, or stupid enough to go back and pretend this hadn't happened. But I knew one thing.

She'd called me, Honey.

And I remembered who I used to be.

Ranch Roots and Rising Tension

THE RADIO CRACKLED AS the old truck rolled down the highway, windows half-cracked and the smell of hay clinging to the seats. The air was warm—not heavy, just enough spring in it to make the breeze feel as if it was brushing off dust that settled on me years ago. Olivia drove like she always had—one hand on the wheel, the other resting loose on the windowsill, thumb tapping against the metal as she hummed along with some Miranda Lambert song. Her braid hung over her shoulder, a strand of red hair whipping against her cheek, and she didn't bother fixing it.

I didn't say much, not at first. It was enough to be out, enough to have gotten away with it, twice in one week, without suspicion. I'd said I was going back to the grocery store, made a second list, even tore up the receipt from yesterday, just in case he checked. The lies had come easier this time. That scared me more than anything.

We passed the turnoff to the high school, the same road I used to take on my bike when I was fourteen and thought denim jackets made me look like a grown-up. The gas station with the busted pump still hadn't been fixed. I stared out the window, watching the landscape flatten into grazing land and rough pasture, the kind of view that used to make me roll my eyes because I thought it was boring.

"You hungry?" Olivia asked, not looking at me.

I shook my head. "I'm okay."

She glanced over. "You ate anything today?"

"I had toast."

"That's not eating."

"I didn't feel like more."

She didn't push it. Just let the silence return, but softer this time.

The road dipped and curved, gravel pinging against the undercarriage. We passed a weather-worn barn with a sun-faded sign for apples and honey that probably hadn't been open for years. I recognized it. We used to dare each other to sneak inside in the summers. I'd backed out every time. Olivia never had.

My hand rested on my knee, fingers twitching when I saw the split-rail fence come into view. The gate had always leaned to one side, like it couldn't quite hold its own weight. It still did. A rusted sign swung crooked on the post: Rustlers Ridge Ranch.

She slowed down, pulling off to the side, tires crunching into the gravel lot. The engine cut, and the quiet was sudden. Wind carried the faint sound of horses from somewhere out back, distant hooves clopping on dirt.

"Figured we'd stop here before heading to High Plains," Olivia said. "Didn't want to just drive by."

My chest tightened. "You sure it's okay?"

She turned to me, one brow raised. "Honey, your name is still on half the fence posts out there. This place loved you before you ever left it."

I looked out across the open space. The main barn was still standing, though the roof sagged more than I remembered. The red paint was chipped, the doors warped. But the corral was still intact, the troughs lined along the fence. I could just make out a horse in the distance, swishing its tail, head low.

"You want to walk a bit?"

My hand hovered over the door handle before pulling it open. Gravel shifted beneath my boots as I stepped down. The smell of dust and hay hit me hard, thick with memories. My legs felt heavy, like the air here knew how long I'd been gone, and wasn't sure I deserved to be back.

We crossed through the open gate, boots thudding against the hard-packed ground. Olivia walked a few feet ahead, letting me set the pace without making it obvious. I stared at the barn windows, cracked and streaked with dirt, the way the roof dipped just like my dad used to complain about. Said the whole damn thing would cave, if someone didn't reinforce the beams. I used to sit up there with my sketchpad, drawing horses that looked more like dogs, dreaming about opening a design studio right here on the ranch someday.

"Looks smaller," I mused.

Olivia turned slightly. "That's how it goes."

"It used to feel huge. Like the sky started from the top of the barn."

"It still kinda does," she said, squinting up.

We walked past the tack shed. The door hung open, a broken hinge clinging to the frame by one stubborn screw. Inside, I spotted an old saddle thrown over a rack, leather dry and curling around the edges. I reached out and brushed it with my fingertips. The texture was rough, stiff. It wasn't the one I used to ride with, but it was close.

"Is that...?"

"Yours got moved to my place," Olivia said. "Figured it deserved better care."

I swallowed and nodded.

We kept walking until the paddock fence rose in front of us, silver-gray slats warm under the sun. The horse I'd seen earlier was closer now, a dappled gray with white around her muzzle.

She ambled toward us, slow and curious. I held my hand out automatically.

"She's gentle," Olivia said. "Retired from trail rides. She likes the company."

I scratched her nose; felt the way she leaned into it. Her eyes were big and soft, blinking slow. My throat clenched.

"I miss this," I said. "I didn't think I did. But I do."

"It never left you."

"I don't even know who I am anymore."

Olivia leaned against the fence. "You're still the girl who ran barefoot across this field screaming at cows."

"That girl wouldn't know what to do with me now."

"She'd know how to fight."

I laughed. "She was all mouth and no backup."

"Maybe. But she didn't take shit from anybody."

I looked out across the field. The sunlight glinted off the metal gate at the far end, and in the distance, the Wasatch peaks sat quiet, watching like they always did. I remembered riding along the tree line, wind whipping through my hair, Lemon screaming at me to slow down before I fell off and cracked something. I hadn't cared. Not back then.

"Tell me what's stopping you," Olivia said, voice low.

I rested my elbows on the top rail; cheek pressed to the warm wood. "Everything. Fear. Habit. I don't know where I'd go. I don't know what I'd even take. He watches everything. My

texts, my steps. Sometimes he doesn't even need to say anything—he just looks at me like he's already made the decision
for both of us."

"He ever stop you from seeing a doctor?"

I flinched. "I haven't tried."

"What about money? You have access?"

"Not really. He lets me buy groceries, nothing else."

She blew a slow breath out. "We can work around all that."

I looked over. "It's not that easy."

"I know it's not. But it's not impossible either."

I stayed quiet, listening to the wind pick up again, tugging
at the edge of my jacket. The horse leaned her head over the
fence, nuzzling Olivia's shoulder. She smiled, reached up, and
scratched behind the mare's ear.

"You want her?" Olivia asked.

I blinked. "What?"

"This horse. She's yours if you want her. Hell, she probably
remembers you better than I do."

I laughed softly. "I wouldn't even know what to do."

"You'd remember."

The horse huffed against my arm, breath warm and steady.
I rested my hand on her forehead, just above her eyes, and
closed mine. Everything inside me ached. Not from pain this
time, but from something more confusing. Longing, maybe.
Or grief, for the girl I used to be. The one who wore boots

caked in mud and climbed fences just to feel taller. The one who had plans.

"I should go," I said eventually. "He'll notice if I'm late."

"You got a plan yet?"

I shook my head. "Not yet."

"Well, start thinking of one. The next time you sneak out, you don't go back."

"I don't know if I'm ready."

"Maybe not. But you're close."

I glanced at her, really looked. Her face was wind-chapped, sun-kissed, eyes tired in the way people's get when they work hard, and love harder. I didn't say thank you. It didn't feel big enough.

We didn't go straight back to the truck. Olivia veered off toward the fence line, where the sun had started to stretch long across the pasture, turning everything gold and low-shadowed. I followed without asking why. We climbed the old fence rail like we used to, knees swinging over the edge, boots hitting wood, shoulders brushing slightly. It groaned beneath our weight, but held. Some things still did.

The field ahead looked the same as it always had—wild and wide, patchy with green and brown where winter still clung to the roots. A few horses dotted the back stretch, heads bent low to graze. One lifted its neck and snorted, ears flicking toward us, then went back to its patch of grass like we weren't worth the trouble.

Olivia didn't rush to fill the air. She let the wind talk first, kicking dust off the road behind us, rustling the sparse leaves that started to come in on the trees that lined the fence.

"You remember how you used to belt out music from that busted iPod?" she asked, eyes trained on the field. "Didn't matter if it was Taylor Swift or Nirvana. You'd make up half the lyrics and sing like God Himself was listening."

I smiled, eyes burning. "I sounded terrible."

"Yeah. That was the best part."

I picked at a splintered edge on the fence, letting it bite into the pad of my thumb. "I used to think if I sang loud enough, everything else would drown out."

"You did. You were loud as hell."

"I used to want to be fearless," I said, barely above a whisper. "Like in those songs."

"You were."

"Not really."

She looked over at me. "You jumped a fence to chase a cow once. You tried to teach your horse to dance. You made Lemon eat a handful of dirt on a dare."

I laughed through my nose. "She never forgave me for that."

"She did. She just kept the story in her back pocket for blackmail."

"She was always smarter."

"You were always bolder."

I stared down at my boots, at the way my jeans creased around the knees. "I used to think yellow meant joy."

"It still does."

"Not for me."

"Why not?"

"It reminds me of what I lost."

"It can remind you of what's still there."

I didn't answer. I just stared out across the pasture, eyes tracing the fence line, following to where it disappeared behind the barn. The sky was starting to turn pink at the edges. That dusky gold kind of light that makes everything look softer than it really is. I used to love this time of day. I used to believe it meant anything could still happen.

"You were going to paint your Jeep yellow once," she said, nudging me with her elbow. "Remember?"

"Yeah. I chickened out."

"No. He talked you out of it."

My chest tightened. "I thought it was compromise."

"He told you yellow was tacky. You said, 'Well, maybe I'll go with silver then.' Like silver was some kind of consolation prize."

"He said, it was more mature."

"And now?"

"I hate silver."

Olivia sighed and leaned her chin against the top rail, fingers wrapped loose around it. "You used to make me believe the world was bigger than Grantsville."

"God, I was so full of shit," I said, laughing bitterly.

"No. You just weren't scared yet."

I stayed quiet. The sun dipped lower.

"You think she's gone," she said, after a long pause.

"Who?"

"That girl."

"She is."

"She isn't." Her voice was firmer now. "She's just buried under all the quiet."

My throat went tight. I blinked fast.

"She's still in there. Waiting."

"She's tired."

"So are you."

I looked at her, really looked. Her face had that same fierce kind of softness it always had—like she'd punch a guy in the mouth for hurting you, but still cry over a horse movie. She didn't flinch away from my stare. Just let me have it.

"I don't know how to go back," I said.

"Don't. Go forward."

I wiped my eyes with the back of my hand. "I'm scared."

"I know."

"And I'm not strong, like you think."

"You don't have to be strong all at once. You just have to start moving."

"I don't know where I'd even go."

"You already came here. That's a start."

I looked back out at the pasture. One of the horses had come closer, a big chestnut mare with a white blaze across her face. She stood at the edge of the fence now, ears forward, watching us like she was waiting for something.

"She used to be yours," Olivia said. "Well—your family's. But she followed you like a puppy back then."

"I remember."

"She remembers you."

I reached out, touched the top rail again, hand shaking slightly. "I miss this."

"You can have it again."

"I don't deserve it."

"You survived. That's enough."

The sky turned darker, the clouds streaked purple and orange. The last bits of daylight clung to the tops of the mountains like they didn't want to let go yet. Neither did I.

"I think I forgot who I was," I said.

"Then let's remember her."

"She was loud."

"She was bright."

"She was stupid."

"She was brave."

I closed my eyes. The breeze shifted, brushing my cheek like the kind of touch that doesn't hurt.

"You think I could ever be her again?"

"I think you already are. You're just tired from pretending you're not."

I let that settle, let the silence fill the cracks. I didn't need to argue. She wasn't trying to win anything. Just hold a mirror up to something I hadn't seen in a long time.

"I want to ride again," I said suddenly. "Just once."

Olivia didn't smile big. Just gave a quiet nod. "You will."

"And I want to laugh without looking over my shoulder."

"You will."

"And I want to wear yellow again."

"Then wear it."

I bit my lip and stared down at my hands.

"We can take the mare out tomorrow," she said, casual like she wasn't offering me something sacred. "Just a short ride. I'll walk beside you. You don't have to do anything fancy."

"I don't have riding boots anymore."

"Borrow mine."

"I don't—"

She turned her head. "Don't start."

I smiled, just barely.

The chestnut nickered softly, pressing her head against the fence rail. I reached out and ran my hand down her face. Her coat was soft and warm as she leaned into my palm like she remembered.

"I need to go soon," I whispered. "He'll be expecting me."

"I hate that," Olivia muttered.

"Me too."

We sat there a little longer, neither of us speaking. The sun slipped behind the hills, and the field dipped into twilight. I could still smell the horses. Still feel the wood grain under my palms. Still hear the way my heart started to beat like it wasn't afraid to exist.

She finally stood, brushing off her jeans. "Come back soon."

"I will."

"No—really come back. Don't just stop by to pretend."

I stood too, nodding. "Okay."

She walked me to the truck, and I slid into the passenger seat. The engine rumbled to life, headlights cut across the gravel. As we pulled away, I looked back once, watching the barn fade into the shadows, the horse still standing at the fence like she was waiting for me to change my mind.

Maybe next time, I would.

Saddle Up for Freedom

We met again the following Wednesday—same café, same table, tucked into the corner where the sun made everything look warmer than it really was. I'd told him I was going back for toothpaste. The last tube had plenty left, but I said the cap cracked, showed him the split and said it leaked. He barely looked up from his phone. Just grunted and tossed me a crumpled twenty. That was enough.

Olivia was already there when I walked in, nursing a black coffee that smelled burnt from across the room. She looked up, saw me, and smiled like this whole thing wasn't delicate and scary as hell. Like it was normal. Like I wasn't lying to the man who kept my world locked down tighter than any door ever could.

I slid into the seat across from her, dropped my purse into my lap, and tucked my hands around the paper coffee cup I'd grabbed on the way in. It was too hot to sip. My fingers burned, and I liked it.

"You good?" she asked, scanning my face.

I nodded. "Yeah. No questions this morning."

"He ask for a receipt?"

"He didn't even ask what I was buying."

"Then we've got room to move."

Her voice was calm, measured. Like she was planning something boring and technical instead of trying to extract me from my own goddamn prison.

She reached under the table and pulled out a small canvas tote. It looked like any grocery bag from the farmers market—plain, off-white, fraying slightly at the seams. She unzipped it halfway and tilted it toward me.

Inside were folded clothes. A pair of boots. Socks. A sweatshirt. Toothpaste. A backup phone. My heart skipped hard against my ribs.

"You'll keep this in the floorboard of my truck," she said. "Wrapped in a horse blanket. Nobody looks under those."

I swallowed. "What about the phone?"

"Deactivated for now. Once you're out, we'll connect it under a different name."

"You've done this before?"

"Enough to know the rules."

I stared at the bag, hands itching to touch it, to confirm it was real.

"What else?" I asked.

She sat back and took a slow drink from her mug. "Cash. You said he lets you handle groceries, right?"

I nodded.

"You can ask for cash back at the register—small bills. Keep it under twenty at a time. Less than ten is better. Stuff it in your coat pocket, not your wallet. Hide it somewhere in the Jeep where he won't check."

I nodded again, heart racing. "Glove box?"

"Too obvious. Try behind the fuse panel or under the floor mat."

"I can do that."

We fell quiet for a second. I stared out the window while she stirred the coffee she never put sugar in. A woman passed with a baby in a stroller, humming something tuneless under her breath. The baby kicked its feet and squealed at a pigeon.

"I deleted our last thread of messages last night," I said.

"Smart."

"He checks my phone sometimes when I'm sleeping. Not every night. But enough."

"You have a code?"

"He knows it."

Olivia's jaw tightened. "You need to get him off that phone."

"I've tried. He says if I've got nothing to hide, it shouldn't matter."

Her eyes didn't soften. "Next time, drop it down the sink. Say the faucet slipped. Water damage buys us a clean slate."

"I'll think about it."

"You don't have to think. Just nod."

I let out a slow breath and nodded.

The next thirty minutes were planning—quiet, sharp, no room for panic. Olivia laid it all out, step by step, each piece small enough I could manage it without breaking.

Clothes in the truck.

Cash in the floorboard.

Phone plan ready.

I'd need to time it when he was at work, or maybe when he was out drinking after. I couldn't leave mid-argument or during a silent treatment. He had a sixth sense for things I hadn't even done yet. If I flinched wrong, if I looked too calm or too scared, he'd sniff it out.

I told Olivia that too.

She didn't blink. "Then we make sure you're unreadable. You're already good at that."

I cracked a half smile. "Practice makes perfect."

Her hand landed on mine across the table, firm and grounding. "You've survived this long. Now you get to choose what you do with that skill."

The drive back to town was quiet. She dropped me near the edge of the grocery lot, where I could walk across and make it look real. I kept my grocery bag light—milk, eggs, crackers, just enough to show I'd gone. I paid in cash and asked for seven back. Folded it into my palm before I left the store. Slid it under the passenger mat before I turned the Jeep key.

It felt like smuggling treasure. My palms wouldn't stop sweating the whole drive back. My breath stayed shallow, eyes flicking to the rearview mirror more than usual.

When I walked in the front door, he barely looked up from the recliner. The TV was playing something loud and stupid. His beer sat sweating on the end table. He had one sock off, foot propped up, remote clutched like a weapon.

"You get everything?"

I held up the bag. "Yeah."

He reached in, pulled out the crackers, looked at them like he'd forgotten he liked them.

"You didn't get the kind with rosemary again, right?"

"No. Just sea salt."

"Good."

I nodded and moved to the fridge, put things away methodically. He watched me for a minute, then turned back to the screen.

That night, I tucked the second ten-dollar bill into the hollow part of the broom handle in the laundry room. Unscrewed the cap. Slipped it inside. Screwed it back tight.

Small wins.

Three days later, Olivia left an envelope under the seat. Just a card inside that said, "Keep going." No name. No message. A fifty was tucked behind it.

I slid it into an old mason jar and buried it in the backyard; near the dogwood tree we never watered. Told him I was weeding. He barely grunted from the couch.

The hardest part wasn't hiding the things.

It was hiding the hope.

I was used to disappearing in front of him. Used to shrinking my voice, nodding instead of speaking, apologizing for things I didn't do. But now, I had something to protect. A plan. A crack of light. And I had to keep it secret, like it might vanish if he looked at me too hard.

I timed everything. Started keeping track of when he left, how long he stayed gone. I watched for patterns. If he drank after work, I had more hours. If he skipped the bar, I had to stay alert. If he came home with flowers, I braced.

By the end of the week, I'd moved three outfits into Olivia's truck, hidden sixty-eight dollars total, and practiced keeping my face blank—even when I wanted to scream.

At night, I lay on the far edge of the bed with my back to him, staring at the ceiling, whispering every detail to myself like a prayer.

Boots in the floorboard.

Cash in the jar.

Blank phone in the bag.

A way out.

And slowly, something else started to come back.

I stopped flinching every time the front door slammed.

I stopped checking the clock every five minutes when he was late.

I stopped waiting for his moods to decide what kind of day I'd have.

I started reclaiming pieces of myself. I rearranged the kitchen drawers—quietly—put things back where I liked them. I put a single yellow sticky note inside the kitchen cabinet where he'd never look. It said, "Soon."

And for the first time in a long damn while, I believed it.

We'd fallen into a quiet rhythm at home. I avoided him as much as I dared—moving slowly through rooms, serving dinner earlier so I could retreat before the slope of his shadow filled the space. I pretended every day was normal, but inside me something changed. Small rebellions: I locked the bathroom door when I showered. I lingered a little longer at the window, watching clouds cross the sky. I made decisions—quiet ones—just for myself again.

I started planning my departure in small bursts of courage. I sketched out groceries for the week, deliberately choosing items I could pay for in cash and slip some small bills into my coat pocket—as "cash back." I kept the rest in the old mascara tube hidden under the sink. Every time he barked questions about purchases or receipts, I nodded and said "yes, I got everything you wanted," holding a smile even when he looked past it. My hands shook sometimes as I stuffed the big bills in my pocket, but I did it—he never noticed.

Each day I managed a sliver of freedom—no matter how small. I dusted off the interior lining of the Jeep myself now, lining it with old blankets and tucking in my caboodle from the tote stash — the spare phone, the backup clothes, the toothpaste and deodorant. I copied the dusty outline of my logo from Haven & Harmony Interiors onto a napkin, drew the arches of my favorite shade of yellow, reminding myself I once had a business. I blew the napkin out the window into the driveway one morning and felt something inside me stretch.

He'd stop by room doors with his phone in hand, scrolling, checking my messages. But I'd learned to delete any sign of Olivia after every meeting—ruthlessly wiping threads, clearing history. I practiced walking past him without glancing. I kept answers short. When he said, "Tell me what you're up to," I'd shrug, "Just tidying the house," and tuck my chin slightly so he had to look at me anyway.

He hadn't hit me anymore—not yet—but the fear was always there. A cold drum of adrenaline when the front door echoed too loud, or the night was too still. Some nights, I curled under the thin blanket, held my wrist where the old bruise had faded, my breath shallow but steady. At least I knew how to breathe again.

I began to imagine choices beyond survival. At first it felt impossible—a stranger's dream. But each choice made the next one slightly less impossible. I allowed myself to think: where would I go if I left? Olivia's ranch. Provo. Salt Lake. A studio where I could design again under a name that felt like me. I pictured driving the Jeep, top down, yellow shining in the sunlight, singing too loud with the windows open.

Then: when would I leave? I'd learned his rhythm. If he stayed late drinking or took Saturdays off work, that was my window. Mondays at the gym were good too—he claimed that time for himself. I marked these less dangerous slots on a mental calendar, mapping routes, backup escape plans: trust fund acre-grab, quiet motel stay, calling Lemon first thing morning.

He questioned me less often these days. Maybe he assumed the silence meant submission. But I was done shrinking. I shifted drawers, re-organized the spice rack, even moved my yellow sweater to the front of the closet. I justified it to myself as "preparing the house for sale." I swapped coffee mugs I'd cracked for neater ones, but I kept one bright yellow one inside the top cupboard—hidden but waiting.

In the evenings I practiced smiling to myself in the mirror, a steady unbroken grin I could use when he glared. I practiced saying "I'm fine," with enough firmness the words tasted true in my mouth. I practiced silence too—looking into his eyes when he stared across the table, absorbing his questions without blinking, like the answer within me was bigger than his assumptions.

One afternoon while he was glued to a game on the TV, I took my savings jar—the one hidden in the backyard—and counted it. Seventy-four dollars. Enough for a tank of gas, enough to start. I taped the jar in the tote with the extra shoes and set it in the seat of the Jeep, where it wouldn't jostle but was ready to go. My lungs felt tight during the count, but my fingers didn't shake.

At night I lay awake, tracing the outline of the ceiling, mapping the minute of departure in my head. I imagined zippering the tote shut, stepping into running shoes by the door, the rumble of shoes on gravel, the hum of the Jeep engine. I imagined breathing in the dark sky for the last time in this house.

A few days later, when I finally committed, I realized just how many small decisions had lined the path. I hesitated—not from fear alone, but because it felt overwhelming. Then, I remembered Olivia's words: you don't have to do it all at once. I could move forward in increments. And I did.

The day I told him I was going to run errands; I drove to the feed store instead of the grocery. Got a small feed bag, carried it out to the Jeep, layered one of my sweaters on the passenger seat. He didn't look in the window. I carried the tote into the truck bed after dark so no one saw. My pulse hammered, but I forced calm. I was storing tools for the final step, for the day I broke loose.

That night, when he sat on the couch and asked me where I was putting my groceries, I said: "In the back." He nodded, didn't turn. I refused to flinch.

Behind my eyes something shifted—from surviving to choosing. Fear still stalked me, but I had quiet roads laid in my mind. I had plans, clothes packed, phone unlisted. I had names scribbled in the tote and a future in my gut. It didn't feel safe—not yet. But it felt right.

And for the first time in years, I let myself believe that maybe—maybe—I didn't have to live in survival mode anymore. That I could carve a life out of choices I made. That I could be the person who chose joy again, who chose yellow again.

Facing the Mirror

I locked the bathroom door and turned the faucet on, letting it run just loud enough to muffle anything. It didn't need to be hot. I wasn't here to bathe. I stared at the fog-less mirror; at the face I'd learned not to look at directly for too long. The reflection didn't lie—it didn't tell the whole truth either. There were shadows under my eyes I hadn't earned from sleepless nights alone, not really. There was a split at the corner of my lip from where I'd bitten it too hard while smiling through his sarcasm. The skin along my cheekbone still held the faintest greenish bruise, like a fingerprint faded into watercolor.

I touched it gently, before dropping my hand.

The woman in the mirror looked like me, but she didn't hold herself like I used to. Her shoulders curled inward. Her jaw clenched too tight. Her eyes didn't sparkle—they scanned. She wasn't fragile, not truly, but she looked like someone who'd forgotten how to stand tall without asking permission first.

I dragged the little notepad from under the sink, the one I usually used for writing down things we needed from the store. I ripped off the first clean page and sat on the toilet lid, pressing it against my thigh to steady my hand. The pen felt heavy as I uncapped it. I stared at the blank page for a while before writing anything down.

He told me, I was too emotional.

That one felt obvious. Easy. I kept going.

He made fun of my Jeep. Called it a Barbie car.

He told me my designs were *"girly"* and no one would pay for them.

He called me dumb when I spilled coffee on his blueprints.

He laughed when I cried then said it was a joke.

He took my keys when I wanted to leave.

He went silent for a full week when I forgot to defrost the steak.

He told me I was lucky someone like him loved me.

He made me quit my job because he said men wouldn't respect me if I was still working with clients.

He shoved me against the fridge.

He hit me.

He bought flowers after.

I stopped writing, hand cramping. I read it over once, then twice. The words bled through the page, pressed too hard, like I was trying to carve them into something permanent. My throat itched. My eyes burned.

I flipped to a second sheet and kept going.

He deleted my Facebook.

He blocked my sister's number.

He laughed when I cried after I saw the note Lemon sent through the mail and told me to "get over it."

He told me I'd never survive on my own.

He said, no one would believe me.

He said I was too sensitive, too dramatic, too much.

And then, when I was quiet—he said, I was cold. Emotionless. A bitch.

The list ran halfway down the second page when the pen stopped working. I shook it, pressed harder. Nothing. I let it drop into the sink.

I stared at what I'd written, pages trembling slightly in my hands, then folded them in half. I held them over the trash can and hesitated.

It felt wrong to throw them out. Like I was letting them win. But keeping them felt heavier. Like anchoring the ugliest parts of him to me again. I needed to see them, to write them out. But I didn't need to carry them.

I tore the first sheet straight down the middle, then again into quarters. Then the second page. I kept ripping until the words were gone. Until the pieces were just scraps. Then I flushed them. One batch, then another.

The sound echoed in the small bathroom.

I sat back on the lid again and stared at my lap.

It didn't fix anything. It didn't erase the years I gave him, or the bruises I covered up with makeup, or the stretch of silence I'd let curl around my spine like a vice. But it helped. A little.

I felt lighter. Not free. But lighter.

That night, he wanted sex. I pretended to be asleep. He climbed into the bed too hard, tugged at the sheets like he meant to yank them out from under me. My stomach flipped, but I didn't move. I kept my eyes closed, breathing slow and even. He didn't touch me. Just laid there, fuming.

In the morning, he slammed the bathroom door. Didn't say goodbye. That was fine.

I used the time to move another fifty dollars into Olivia's glove compartment. I drove to the bank under the excuse of checking on my account for a refund that never existed. The teller gave me no trouble when I asked for cash. I wrapped it inside a tampon box, slid the box into my tote, and smiled politely as I left.

The fear never left my chest, but it lived beside something else now—a steady thrum that reminded me I was doing this. I was actually doing it.

I started noticing the little ways I'd stopped apologizing. I poured myself a second cup of coffee without asking. I hummed while folding laundry. I put my yellow hoodie back on the hook by the front door, bold as brass. It hadn't been out in months.

He didn't comment, but I caught him looking at it once.

I didn't look away.

At night, I started journaling again. Just a few lines, things I wanted to remember:

I want to see Lemon again. I miss her laugh. I miss how she made breakfast while dancing.

I want to design a space that feels like me again—soft light, bookshelves, velvet cushions, a record player spinning old jazz.

I want to wear yellow without shame.

I want to breathe without measuring it first.

I want to be mine again.

I folded those pages too, but not into pieces. I kept them. Slipped them behind the mirror in my old jewelry box, next to a photo of my parents I'd almost thrown away last year when I couldn't handle how disappointed they'd look.

The next time Olivia picked me up, she didn't ask if I was ready. She just handed me a coffee, and we drove back to the ranch.

I told her about the list. About flushing it.

She nodded. "Good."

"You think it's dumb?"

"I think it's strong."

"It didn't feel strong. It felt…" I paused. "Like dragging my own ghosts into the light."

"Maybe that's the point."

We didn't say much else. We rode horses that day—just slow and easy through the pasture while the sun dipped low. She didn't push. I didn't explain. We just existed, side by side, without fear or silence or rules.

When she dropped me off that evening, I sat in the Jeep longer than I needed to. The house lights were off. He wasn't home yet. I could hear dogs barking faintly two blocks over. Somewhere, someone grilled something that smelled like actual peace.

I climbed out, slow and steady, and locked the Jeep behind me.

Inside, I moved like normal. Dinner reheated. Couch fluffed. I even changed into leggings and washed my face before he walked in.

He smelled like beer and sweat.

"Where were you?" he asked.

"Target."

"What'd you get?"

"Face wash and a dish towel."

He grunted. "Dinner?"

"In the microwave."

He didn't say thank you. Didn't need to. I didn't wait around for praise anymore.

While he ate, I sat in the hallway with a book in my lap. I didn't read it. I just watched the words and thought about tomorrow. About where I'd hide the next ten dollars. About how many days I had left before I'd finally walk out the front door and never come back.

Not long now.

Pieces of Me

I pulled into Lemon's driveway just after noon, the sun high and warm above the Wasatch peaks. My stomach knotted—anticipation, dread, hope—all tangled together. I turned off the Jeep, took a breath, and slipped the spare key from under the mat where the flower pot used to sit. Quiet steps on the porch floorboards, then I paused at the door. I didn't know what to expect. Anything could shift between a knock and an answer.

The door swung open before I even raised my hand.

"Look who finally decided to show up," my sister said, voice sharp and teasing, face bright with surprise. Her red hair was coiled loose at the nape of her neck, a few strands escaping like they didn't care.

"Honey," she said, all at once. She stepped aside, gave me room to breathe. "Blowing through here like you own the place."

I laughed—nervous and small. "Thought I'd drop by before you thought I ghosted for good."

She narrowed her eyes. "You owe me a good excuse, Sunshine—or at least better juice."

I stepped inside and she closed the door behind me like we were picking up where we left off. Kitchen smelled like coffee, and something baked. The living room looked the same, except for a new throw on the couch. That used to be mine. I registered that, smiled inwardly.

"Well? Come in," Lemon said. "Sit at the table. I made sandwiches and cold tea."

I followed the sound of the fridge humming, found her in the kitchen slipping food into paper bags. She tossed one over her shoulder. "Turkey, cheese, avocado, yours with hummus. No mustard—didn't trust you this time."

I grinned as I sat at the patio table, outside under the shade of the awning. The mountains rolled bluish in the distance. She brought over two iced teas—sweet, pale amber, condensation slid down the glass. I held mine tight; my fingers turned cold despite the heat and took a sip.

"Nice timing," she said, pulling her chair close. "Talk about dramatic arrivals."

"We've all had our road trips," I said.

She raised an eyebrow. "Yeah? What changed?"

"I realized I was missing out on a lot." I reached across and squeezed her hand. "I missed you."

She stared for a second, then smiled, small and honest. "Good to know Tea Girl is still alive."

I laughed again. The ache in my chest loosened. We dug into the sandwiches without ceremony. I closed my eyes and tasted avocado, cheese, turkey. Normal flavors. I realized how much ordinary things had escaped me.

She leaned back, elbows on the table. "Remember when you filled my shoes with shaving cream at my wedding?"

I pushed my hair behind my ear. "You had it coming."

"You mean for making me hold *your* tote bag on the dance floor? Yeah, I had it coming."

We traded stories—like thieves trading stolen gems—about broken fences, stolen donuts from Almond's, rival sponge wars in the kitchen. I pointed to the mountain range. "We used to hike one of those trails after school."

"You always dragged me along," she said. "Said, I'd thank you someday."

"I never did."

"Yeah, you booked the wrong sister for encouragement."

I sighed. "I screwed up, Lemon."

"Like some guy blew some wind through your hair kind of screwed up?" She smirked.

"You deserve better than some excuse."

Her tone softened. "I'm just happy you're here now."

We finished tea and sandwiches, leaving napkins scrunched and crumbs unattended. Lemon rose, stacked bags, and I offered to help. She waved it away.

I stood at the edge of the porch while she cleared. I looked out at the mountains, breathing in that crisp air, like maybe I could tether a piece of peace there. She returned carrying plates and napkins. Set them in the bag without ceremony—as if nothing was broken.

"You staying long?" she asked, wiping the table briskly.

I padded up beside her. "Only until Austin gets off work."

She nodded. "Clever."

I picked one of the plates from the bag and held it. My hands hummed with something steady.

"How are you doing?" she asked, not meeting my eyes.

"Alright." I folded into myself. "Work's fine. I'm okay."

She nodded again, scrubbing at the wood lightly. "Good."

We stalled like that for a second. I stared out, she stared at the plates.

Shadows moved across the distant peaks with the sun's descent. The afternoon light shifted, golden and soft. I tucked a few loose strands behind my ear.

"Thanks," I said.

She turned just enough. "For coming."

I nodded. "Sorry it took me this long."

She smiled like she believed me. "Anytime."

The porch went quiet again, not heavy. Just easy. The kind of moment that knows if you pair it with the past, it always fits.

I slid the dirty plates into the sink with her. Next to the battered red pitcher we used to juggle during summers. I rinsed crumbs, set the sponge aside. Felt something shift—lighter.

Lemon dried the last plate with a ragged old dish towel and set it on the rack beside me. I leaned against the counter; arms crossed over my stomach like I could hold myself together with just pressure and quiet.

The porch door creaked open with a push of her hip, and she stepped outside without a word. I followed her a few seconds later, letting the screen fall shut behind me. The air was cool now, crisp with the kind of chill that hinted fall wasn't far off. The sky stretched wide above the mountains, stained amber and lavender. We leaned against the railing like we used to when we were kids, back when we'd whisper secrets and dares in the dark.

I watched the last of the light disappear behind the ridgeline and cleared my throat.

"I need to tell you something."

Lemon didn't say anything. Just turned her head, waiting.

"I didn't stop calling because I was busy. Or because I didn't care."

Her brows lifted just barely. "I figured that out."

"He made me stop. Little by little. It wasn't, like, one day he said I couldn't talk to you. It was more like... every time I mentioned you, he'd make a comment. Roll his eyes. Say you were trying to stir shit up. That you didn't respect boundaries."

Lemon snorted once under her breath, but didn't interrupt.

"Then it was comments about the time I spent texting. Then deleting contacts from my phone. Then telling me who I should be around and who I shouldn't. Eventually I just... stopped arguing. It was easier."

I felt my jaw tighten. My hands fidgeted against the porch rail, fingers cold even though the evening was mild.

"I thought it was normal. That couples just kind of become each other's whole world. I didn't realize he was cutting me off from mine."

Her head tilted slightly. Her face didn't change much, but I knew that look. It was the one she gave when she was absorbing everything and holding her tongue until I was ready.

"He hit me," I said, plain. The words dropped from my mouth like dead weight. "It wasn't just yelling. It started with shoving. Doors slammed. Silence when I made a wrong move.

Then the first time he slapped me; I stood there and told myself it didn't hurt. Like if I just said it enough, it would be true."

I pulled back the collar of my shirt and showed her the faint greenish-yellow bruise still clinging to my shoulder. She looked at it, then up at me. Didn't flinch. Didn't gasp. Just looked.

"That's not the only one," I said quietly. "It's never consistent. Sometimes it's a shove. Sometimes he throws things near me but not at me. Says I'm too sensitive. Says I push him to it."

Lemon's hand reached out and rested on the rail beside mine. Not touching, just close.

"I started making lists," I continued, almost like I was confessing. "Every insult. Everything he said that twisted me up. I wrote it all down in this notebook I kept inside an old cereal box. I tore it up a few weeks ago, flushed it, but I memorized most of it. I had to."

"Olivia found me at Salt City Brews. Called me Honey, and I cried right there with a damn muffin in my hand. I hadn't heard that name in so long, it felt like hearing it for the first time."

I rubbed my fingers together, grounding myself. "She's helping me leave. Slowly. I've been moving clothes into her truck, hiding cash, figuring out when he's at work and when I have windows. She checks in with me every couple days, makes sure I'm safe. I'm planning it carefully, so he doesn't catch on."

"Does he still check your phone?"

"Every day," I said. "I delete messages from her as soon as I read them. I call her from the grocery store bathroom, not from home. I've got a backup phone hidden in the lining of my old yellow gym bag under the bed."

"Jesus." Her voice cracked just enough to hear the anger behind it, though she didn't raise it.

"I'm not telling you this so you'll fix it. Or because I want you to feel guilty. I just—" I cut myself off, swallowing. "I need you to understand why I disappeared. I didn't want to."

"I knew something was wrong," she said finally. "I didn't know what exactly. But I knew that wasn't you. You never just go quiet like that. And he always gave me a bad feeling."

"I'm sorry," I said.

"You don't need to be."

"I should've reached out."

"You were scared."

I looked down at the boards beneath our feet. A breeze pushed through the porch, carrying the smell of pine and something earthy and cool.

"I missed you," I said.

"Yeah, well." Her voice softened. "I missed you too. Even if you were being a dumbass."

That made me laugh, short and sharp. "I deserved that."

"Damn right."

I wiped my eyes with the sleeve of my sweatshirt. "I forgot what it was like to talk to someone without calculating everything I said."

"You don't have to do that here."

We fell quiet for a while, the sky deepening to a dusky navy. The air shifted as the last of the sun dropped behind the ridge. Porch lights flicked on across the yard. Lemon stood and stretched her arms overhead.

"You staying longer?"

I shook my head. "I've got to beat him home. He gets suspicious if I'm late."

She nodded. No questions. Just understanding.

We walked back inside. I helped her clean the kitchen, rinsing plates and wiping the counter while she wrapped up the leftover takeout. The domestic rhythm of it felt foreign and comforting at the same time. We didn't talk much, but the silence didn't feel dangerous—it felt like home.

As she placed the last container in the fridge, I paused at the sink, staring out the window above it. The sky was almost black now. Stars just starting to wink into view over the peaks.

"You know where I am," she said behind me. "Whenever."

I nodded, heart tight.

"Don't wait too long."

"I won't."

I left with my keys in one hand and a promise folded in the other—silent, but solid. I climbed into the Jeep, glanced once at the house before pulling out, and whispered to myself on the drive home, just loud enough to hear it over the tires on gravel.

"I'm getting out."

Weight on Your Heart

I SLIPPED INTO THE driveway before sunrise, the grass brushing cold against my ankles. Dawn had yet to break, the sky still dark and quiet, the world holding its breath, like I was. I let the door click behind me and held it—breath pressed tight—until I heard the latch slide into place. That "click" meant more than a door closing; it was permission to begin.

I didn't head for the Jeep. Trusting a vehicle in his name felt too risky. Instead, I hugged my duffel to my chest—clothes, boots, my sketchbook, and a hidden envelope with cash—and climbed silently into Olivia's old blue pickup, where I'd stashed it the night before. The smell of hay and leather was faint but calming, like the promise of home I'd buried under months of survival.

Olivia slid in beside me, her hair in that messy braid I remembered from summers at Rustlers Ridge Ranch. She didn't say anything. Just gave me a look—equal parts steady and soft—and started the engine without a fuss.

We didn't talk as she backed the truck into the street, then steered us toward Grantsville. Just like that, I was moving away from what he controlled. Every mile felt like something giving way inside me. My knuckles went white on the seatbelt latch.

"Coffee?" she murmured, barely above the hum of the truck.

I nodded, throat dry. Couldn't speak yet.

We rolled toward High Plains Pasture—just outside town—but driving past the withered sunflower field I used to ride through hit me unexpectedly. A flutter in my chest, like seeing a ghost. I looked straight ahead and swallowed it down.

We pulled into the barnyard where I'd spent so many sunrises and summers. The corral gate stood waiting, just as it had when I left Gifts of Grass riding lessons behind. The ground crunched under the tires as we eased to a stop.

"So," she said, cutting the engine. "You ready?"

My legs went weak. I pressed both hands to the seatback until they didn't shake anymore. Then I nodded once.

The cold dawn air slipped inside the cab as I climbed out. I could feel the chill all the way to my bones, but I stood taller looking at the barn. It was rougher now—roof sagging, paint peeling—but unchanged in purpose. Safe.

I took a breath and opened the door to the pasture side. Horses came into focus along the fence line, breathing out misty snorts. My heart thrummed. I held the duffel more tightly.

Olivia leaned out the window. "Take your time."

I walked slowly across the gravel path, boots crunching. My stomach felt like a hive. Even so, I kept moving forward, toward the fence where the mare stood waiting—chestnut coat shining like memory, eyes soft as moonlight. I pressed my palm to the rail and closed my eyes.

She whinnied. I rubbed the wood, feeling the grain uneven and warm. I dared to breathe deeper.

"She remembers you," Olivia said behind me, watching quietly. "She came for you right away."

I managed a breathless laugh. "Of course she did."

We walked toward the barn together. I wiped dust off the saddle rack, traced the curves of the leather I once filled with confidence. My knuckles went over old scratches I earned climbing posts as a kid. It was all still here.

Olivia put her hand on my shoulder. I flinched, then let her hold it steady. No expectation, just presence.

"I'm scared," I admitted quietly, head facing the pasture. "But I don't feel lost, not anymore."

"You don't have to go back," she said softly.

"I know."

We saddled the mare together—her hands steady and patient—even though I could barely remember how. I traced the seat straps like I was teaching myself rhythm again.

"She's yours to ride if you want." Olivia's voice was calm. "Or you can just breathe."

I stared at the leather, then at the horse's face. I needed to feel the weight of myself in the world again. I lifted into the saddle with shaky knees, found balance, breathed out, tasted light.

When I slid off, the ache in my thighs was real—but the ache inside me was something else now. A pulse of health.

We sat on the porch afterward, each sipping coffee from chipped mugs. The sun rose behind the mountains, burning gold and honest.

I unpacked the duffel. Laid out the yellow sweater, sketchbook, and jeans cozy with dust. I put on the sweater. The color felt like reclaiming.

Olivia watched with no questions. When I pulled out the backup phone and glanced at it but didn't check it, she nodded.

I ducked my head onto my folded arms over the porch rail. Quiet tears came—not sorrow, not fear, not regret. Just release.

Someone whinnied from the paddock. The chestnut mare looked back toward the barn, then away again. Waiting.

I sat upright.

"Thank you," I whispered.

She'd already turned away, gathering the tack.

I didn't need her to look again. I knew it'd be okay. I slid my sketchbook open and placed it on my lap.

The freedom sky trailed over the ridge, big as all my small steps added together. And right there—feet both in return and departure—I let myself hope.

I sat in the dining room. a tall glass of lemonade sweating in my hands, feeling the chill from the ice on my fingers. The kitchen behind me smelled faintly of mint and lemon zest. Sunlight filtered through lace curtains to dance on the table-cloth. Across from me, Olivia watched quietly, her presence steady like the barn walls outside. My control slipped only once—I sipped, trembled, set the glass down too hard—and that jolt unfolded through my arms like electricity.

A sudden pounding shook the screen door. I froze. Olivia tensed beside me, but she didn't rise—only held her body still. More pounding. The wood and glass rattled.

"Open up!" Austin's voice cut through the panes. "Open the door right now!"

Lemonade spilled on the table. My heart pounded against ribs as if it wanted out. I pressed knees together beneath the table. Olivia stood and moved toward the door with her head high, shoulders squared.

"I tracked her phone," a deep voice growled, low, angry. He was here. Coming to this sanctuary. My hands went numb. I had forgotten the burner phone hidden in my coat pocket. He would find it, call it, locate me.

Olivia's hand gripped the doorknob. She didn't open.

"You think you can hide her from me?" he yelled. "I'm not leaving here without her. She's mine. You got her—why the hell are you pretending?"

Her voice didn't wobble. "You don't have permission. You'll leave. Now."

He kicked—the door didn't crack, but the glass vibrated. My skin prickled. I thought about fleeing, but to where? The barn door? Stables? I crouched and looked out the kitchen's back window, crouched low so he wouldn't see me. My body shook so hard I almost fell to my knees.

"That phone tracked you to here. You want to play games, fine—" His voice fractured. "Where is she?"

Olivia stood firm. I choked on dry air.

"Open the door!"

Olivia didn't move. She reached into her pocket. Calm. Certain. She produced some papers—ownership docs? Something shoved under his nose, maybe a restraining notice. I didn't see, only watched the shift in his posture. Rage taming into confusion.

I held my breath, long enough to taste panic.

"Let me in," he said. "Now."

Her response was crisp: "You need to leave. Now."

He barked something unintelligible. Then thumped against the door once more, before stomping away.

I hugged my knees under the table, head pressed forward, listening for the engine.

He roared off across gravel. The tremors traveled through the ground and up my legs. Olivia sighed softly and turned back toward me, unresolved lines relaxing.

I felt tears well but refused to let them drop. I swallowed hard, eyes raw.

Olivia crouched down and took my hands. They were so cold. "You're safe," she said, steady. "He's gone."

I nodded, mouth dry. My whole body felt like a coiled spring. I opened my eyes and saw the dust trails dissipating outside the window.

I exhaled like I'd swallowed the whole world.

He had clawed his way into a borrowed sanctuary, and demanded me. I realized how close I came to trading freedom for comfort again.

"Oh God," I whispered, voice hoarse. "I left the phone."

I slipped my hand into my pocket—I'd stashed the burner there too, but I'd grabbed the old one out of habit. I pulled out the overlooked phone. It was lit, showing location sharing on.

"Damn it." I flipped it off and planted it under my shoe. With a rough twist I smashed it against the wooden floor until it cracked. Plastic shards and dusty glass scattered.

My body sagged. Reality settled like ice inside me: he'd tracked me, knew where I was, came looking. I had almost failed right there.

Olivia stayed silent. She wiped away the splinters and brushed the plastic back into the bag.

I moved to the window and watched him drive off. He left a painting of dust behind—not like extinction, but like a storm receding. My chest felt squeezed. My faith wavered, then settled: there was no going back.

He couldn't enter—not now. And I could never go back to being silent again.

My reflection stared back through the glass: tousled hair, aching shoulders, eyes that flickered between terror and fire. I realized standing there I wasn't fragile, not the kind he thought I was. I cared about scars too much to ignore what they meant.

I turned away and sank to the floor beside Olivia, leaning into her legs. Her denim held me, no words, just pressure and promise. We stayed curled there while dusk gathered deeper outside and the lights in the house flickered soft and kind.

He might rage or search again. But he wouldn't get to me—not here. I'd left the Jeep, left the house, left the phone. I couldn't risk another tether. The cracked pieces beside me weren't just a broken phone—they were pieces of the ending.

When I finally tumbled off her legs and staggered to my feet, I carried the shattered phone in the bag with me and dropped it in the trash right by the sink. There was no sound.

I left Lemon for tomorrow, ranch for freedom. Fear was still there, loyal and bruised. But courage ran deeper.

When I finally closed my eyes, I didn't dream of him.

I dreamed of sunrise over the pasture, of yellow tops shining, of a house I'd design where I chose who walked through the front door.

That night I slept without waking. Ear pressed against the mattress, breath steady in each rib.

I woke alone, not afraid.

Because now I knew how close I almost came to staying.

And I knew: I would never let that be me again.

Joyride to Nowhere

I STARTED DRIVING WITHOUT really thinking where I was headed. Olivia's old truck smelled faintly of saddle soap and sweet hay. I gripped the wheel, knuckles white, chasing the dash-lit road until the neon glow faded behind me. Barns and gas stations flicked past, faded signs advertising feed, hay, "Cold Beer," "Fix Your Farm Truck." Everything looked familiar and strange—like memories photographed in sepia, edges blurred. I didn't know who I was yet, but I knew I didn't want to go home.

The truck engine hummed through the empty seats. Radio was silent. I flipped the visor mirror closed and stared at my eyes—glassy, red-rimmed—eyes that stung from tears or exhaustion, or maybe both. I pressed my forehead to the steering wheel, feeling how the leather warmed beneath my skin. A wave hit: longing, grief, relief all lodged together in my bloodstream.

I drove past Rustlers Ridge exit, then kept going, passing patchy fields and fence lines where we used to ride. Tears spilled hot and sudden, sliding down my cheeks before I could blink. I couldn't tell if I was crying for what I'd lost—or what I'd finally let go of. I didn't care. I just needed it out.

I pulled onto a dirt side-road and stepped on the brakes. Gravel spat at the tires. The sun hung low against the western sky, cloud-smudged color washing fields in pink and gold. I let the engine idle and closed my eyes again. Hands shook against the wheel. Vision blurred. I leaned forward and sobbed, wet breaths rattling in my chest. It felt like grief for thinking I couldn't leave, relief that I had, fear that I didn't know what came next. I sat there until the tears slowed, my heartbeat softened, until nothing caught in my lungs.

When I opened my eyes, the grass leaned golden in the wind. No trucks. No voices. Only the sky stretching like a silent promise.

I slipped gloves on, reached under the seat for my duffel, grabbed the sketchbook and pencil. I wrote "Freedom" in bold letters across the front page. Sounds stupid, but the pencil felt steady. I traced it three times.

I climbed back in, keyed the ignition, and headed back toward High Plains Pasture. The drive felt quieter than it had been—like my own thoughts pushed away everything extraneous. I passed the feed store, then the corral fence, then the old apple orchard I used to pick through. The trees were bare now, winter waiting. I felt something expand inside my chest.

I pulled up to the ranch house, dust sliding off the tires. Olivia came out, barefoot across the porch—hair loose, jeans rolled—coughing out a laugh when she saw me.

"Thought you ran off for good," she said, arms out.

I stumbled to the edge of her, letting her hold me steady. I'd undone months of fear in the span of minutes. Everything I was afraid to lose—the barn, the mare, the land—I didn't. It still stood. It had waited for me.

We sat at the table again, simple food—soup in bowls, crackers, lemonade. Light shifted through the window. Neither of us said much. A scratchy country station played on a battered speaker: Patsy singing about heartbreak. I watched steam roll across the surface of soup and thought that small comfort was real.

She cleared her throat, nodded to my sketchbook. "Tell me what you wrote."

I flipped open the sketchbook to the page. Under Freedom was doodle, after doodle of yellow flowers, horses, mountains. I showed her. She studied them, then smiled.

"I like these," she said softly.

I traced a horse's muzzle with my finger, memory soft. "It's the first time I sketched without thinking of him."

She nodded. "That's exactly it."

Silence followed, but it didn't feel empty. It felt spacious. I didn't feel fractured. I felt open.

Night came slow. We finished the soup in silence. She washed the dishes. I folded napkins and parted grass from the floor seam of the porch. When the music changed to Dolly, I stood behind a chair and leaned my arms on its back.

She came around and offered me a hug. I didn't move. Just stood there letting her hold me. I closed my eyes and rested my cheek against her shoulder.

I finally slipped onto the couch; legs curled beneath me. She sat beside me, steady.

I stared out the window—dark outside, lights flickering off the corral—and thought how this day shifted something inside me. No drafts of fear. No clattering doubts. Just the low hum of survival's next step.

When I lay down in the guest room, I didn't check the door lock twice. I didn't jump at creaking floors. I didn't flinch at preparing for danger. Because I knew: the worst already happened. The scariest part—the decision to stay—passed.

I fell asleep hard, without wondering if sleep would slip from me again.

I woke hours later to silence and moonlight. Breathing even. Canine breathed quietly outside. Nothing he owned. Nothing he mapped. Just me, breathing flesh and blood, and possibility.

I waited there, counting each breath like I was claiming space. Not for rows of silent treatments, or gaslit nightmares. But for a yellow hoodie in a duffel bag, a sketchbook with scribbled hope, and the knowledge I was free to choose again.

That morning, I'd start sketching the ranch house for restoration, invite Lemon to lunch, call a small client I ghosted a year ago—with a better version of me someone might actually pay.

I slept without dread. And when I woke, it was clear: the road ahead might be rough. But it was mine.

Turning Tables

THE PHONE STARTED RINGING before the kettle even clicked off. I stood there in Olivia's kitchen, hands still on the handle, water just shy of boiling, and the screen lit up like it had something urgent to say. It buzzed once. Then again. Then again. I didn't move. I didn't answer. The caller ID didn't say his name, but it didn't need it to. The number was unfamiliar, but the rhythm—three calls, back-to-back—was his. I knew it, the way you know a bad dream is real even after you've woken up. I stared down at the screen. The kettle screamed.

Olivia walked in, rubbing sleep from her eyes, hair twisted in a knot at the back of her head. She looked at the phone, then at me. Her eyebrows dropped low. "That him?"

I nodded, swallowed the iron taste in my throat.

"You want me to deal with it?"

I didn't answer right away. The phone stopped buzzing, then lit up again with a text. Then another. My fingers curled around the counter top edge. I forced myself to look.

WHERE THE HELL ARE YOU.

You really doing this? You know what this looks like?

You made me lose a week's pay. Hope it was worth it.

Another call. I let it go to voice mail.

He texted again.

You're being dramatic. Just fucking talk to me. We can work this out.

I turned the screen face down and braced my palms flat on the counter. The laminate was cool beneath my skin, the corners worn soft from years of elbows and coffee cups and real conversation—things I hadn't had in a long time. I didn't say a word.

Olivia came around and set her coffee on the table. "We need to block him," she said gently, not pushing but firm. "All of it. Number, email, socials. You don't need to read another word of that shit."

I shook my head. "He's got one of those services—search sites or something. He found this number. He'll keep finding others. He says my leaving made him do it, like it's my fault we're losing money."

She looked me dead-on. "He's just pissed he can't control you anymore."

"I left my Jeep. It's technically his. He could report it stolen. He could twist it."

"He could," she agreed. "But he'd be making noise that people would notice. You're safe here. He knows that."

I didn't feel safe. I felt like a hunted animal that just ducked into the nearest burrow. I nodded anyway. She moved to the phone, knelt beside me, and held out her hand. I hesitated, then gave it to her. She pulled up settings, showed me each step. We blocked the number. I watched as she went through the apps—Instagram, Facebook, email. We changed passwords. We set up a new email, tied to nothing. She added a two-step verification that went through her phone.

"There," she said. "If he keeps pushing, we'll go legal. But I doubt he wants a spotlight on his record."

I didn't answer. I picked up the tea and carried it to the back porch. The mug shook in my hands. I wrapped both palms around it like it could anchor me. Olivia followed, sat across from me in the white wicker chair, blanket around her shoulders.

"He's going to keep trying," I said after a while. "I know him. He'll flip from pissed, to charming, to pissed again. He used to do that when I wanted to visit my sister. He'd get quiet for days, then make some joke about how she thought she was better than us. Then he'd take me out to dinner like he hadn't said anything. Like I should be grateful."

She didn't interrupt. Just sipped her drink and waited.

"He used to tell me my friends weren't really friends. Said they'd talk shit behind my back. Then he said I was lucky he put up with me. That I was a lot. Too loud, too emotional. That no one else would deal with me like he did."

Olivia's jaw worked tight, but her voice was steady. "They always try to isolate first. Makes it easier to make you doubt yourself."

I laughed, but it came out bitter. "I doubted everything. I even doubted whether I remembered things right. If he slammed the door, or was I was being 'dramatic.' If he grabbed my wrist too hard, or I just bruised easy."

"You don't bruise easy," she said. "I've seen the way you take a fall. That one on your shoulder—that's not from bumping a cabinet."

I looked away. The mug warmed my fingers, but nothing inside me felt settled.

She went quiet for a while. Then said, "We're putting everything important in a lockbox. You have your ID?"

"Yeah. Hidden in the lining of my wallet."

"Good. We'll scan a copy too. Birth certificate, social, all of it. We'll keep it here, locked, and back it up. You're not gonna lose yourself again. Not if I can help it."

The words hit something soft and sore. My throat tightened. I nodded once and stared out to the pasture. Horses moved like shadows across the early morning fog. Birds started up in the distance, and somewhere close by, the first crunch of gravel from the ranch hand's truck rolled past.

"He'll twist everything," I finally whispered. "He'll tell people I cheated, or stole, or abandoned him without warning."

"Let him," she said. "The people who matter already know who you are. The ones who believe his version—fuck 'em. They weren't on your side anyway."

I didn't believe that yet, but I wanted to.

Later that afternoon, we set up the lockbox. I printed out old documents, tucked them into folders. We wrote down a list of everything he may still have access to—old email addresses, financial apps, shared streaming services, the bank account I'd already closed. Olivia helped me write out a new budget. We added in food costs, gas for her truck, savings for the future.

"You don't owe me a damn thing," she said when I hesitated. "But I want you to know you can take care of yourself. We'll make sure of that."

That night, another message came through—this time through a weird old group chat I had forgot existed. He'd added a new number.

You're really trying to make me the bad guy. Hope you enjoy playing victim. You think I won't find you? I always find you.

I showed it to her. She didn't flinch. Just pulled the phone from my hand, reported the number, and deleted the chat entirely.

"We're cutting the last wire," she said. "And then we're burning the scissors."

She took me outside after that. The sky was streaked pink and gray. She handed me a small matchbook and a tin bucket. We walked to the edge of the property. She gave me a lighter.

"Write what you want to be done with," she said.

I did, then I tore the paper into pieces. I wrote down every lie he told me that I had swallowed like scripture. Every insult dressed up as advice. Every night I spent convincing myself it was normal. Every time I made myself smaller so he wouldn't erupt.

When I was done, she lit the match.

We watched the flames catch and curl and rise. The paper blackened, cracked, fell into ash. I didn't speak. I didn't cry. But something loosened in my chest. Like my ribs had been holding in a breath for years.

Back inside, we cooked something easy—grilled cheese and soup. We listened to some old rock band she loved. She danced around the kitchen, barefoot, spoon in one hand, hips swaying to the beat. I laughed—it surprised us both.

"See?" she grinned. "You're still in there."

"I don't feel like me yet."

"Doesn't have to be all at once. Just enough to know you're on your way."

We ate on the couch. She showed me a meme on her phone, we laughed. We watched a stupid movie, one where the girl leaves the guy and runs a goat farm. It was cheesy, but when the credits rolled, I felt something real.

After she went to bed, I sat with my last mug of tea and thumbed through my sketchbook. I added more pages—drawings of the ranch, the porch, a boot on the top stair, her dog stretched across the drive. I drew the tin bucket, flames licking through the air.

I wrote one word under it: Done.

My phone stayed silent. No calls. No threats. No apologies twisted into barbed wire.

I curled under the quilt she loaned me and stared at the ceiling until the stars shifted outside the window. And even though fear still coiled somewhere deep in my chest, for the first time in a long time, it wasn't the loudest thing.

The sun had barely stretched past the ridge when Olivia walked into the kitchen and dropped a yellow legal pad on the table with a soft thud. She poured her coffee first, black, steam fogging her glasses, then wordlessly slid the notepad toward me. I blinked at it, still half-asleep, head fuzzy from a night of fractured dreams and phantom notifications which never came.

"What's this?" I asked, voice low and raw.

"A project," she said. "You and me."

I looked down. She'd written one word in blocky capital letters at the top: CONTROL. Underneath, she'd already made the first bullet point: Phone records.

I laughed under my breath, though it didn't sound like humor. "This is gonna be depressing."

"Probably," she said. "But we're doing it anyway."

I wrapped both hands around my mug, bracing against the heat and the truth. I didn't want to look at the list. Didn't want to see it all laid out that clearly. But I also didn't want to be afraid of my own history anymore.

So, I pulled the pad closer and picked up the pen.

"Calendar," I said after a beat. "He'd sync his with mine. Said it was to 'stay connected,' but it meant I couldn't add a nail appointment without explaining why I needed it."

Olivia nodded and added it.

"Who I texted. Who I followed on social media. He'd scroll through my DMs while I slept."

I added: social, texts, private messages.

"Clothes," I muttered, frowning as the memories unspooled. "If I wore something he didn't like, he'd make a joke about how it made me look desperate. Or like I was trying too hard."

I felt my stomach turn as I remembered how I started hiding new purchases, cutting off tags to pretend they were old shirts.

"Add that," I whispered. "Clothing, appearance."

"He ever stop you from seeing someone?" Olivia asked.

I didn't look up. "Everyone. My sister, coworkers he thought were 'too flirty,' my high school friends. Said they were bad influences. Or they made me act weird."

She wrote, isolated from support system.

We kept going. Voice. Laugh. Opinions. He chipped away at each piece until I barely heard myself anymore. I used to have volume. Fire. I used to interrupt people when I got excited, used to leave voice mails that were basically short stories. I used to ramble when I was happy. But slowly, I started censoring my jokes, softening my tone, shrinking.

When the list hit two pages, Olivia looked up. "You've got good recall."

"I had to," I said. "Had to stay ahead of what might piss him off."

We sat in silence for a few minutes. The kettle ticked behind me on the stove. The dog barked once out by the barn, then quieted again. Outside, the fields shimmered green and gold under the morning light, but all I could see were the jagged pieces of him still clinging to me.

"He's not here," she said softly.

I nodded, throat tight.

"Then quit looking over your shoulder like he is."

"I know."

"No, you don't. You still flinch when the landline rings. You check the truck mirror like he's tailing you. I'm not judging you for it. But we've got to name what's real and what's just his ghost in your head."

I stared down at my chipped mug. The tea had gone cold.

"You're right," I said. "I'm trying."

"You don't have to be perfect at it. You just have to promise me you'll keep trying."

I looked at her. Her eyes didn't waver. "Okay."

We taped the list to the fridge. It looked strange there—something so personal and ugly hanging between the spaghetti recipe, and a magnet shaped like a cow. But every time I walked by, it reminded me what wasn't mine anymore. And what I could take back.

The first thing I tackled was my voice.

"I want to start painting again," I told her that afternoon. We were mucking out the stalls behind the barn, boots thick with mud and manure, sweat crawling between my shoulder blades.

She didn't miss a beat. "Good."

"I don't have supplies."

"I've got a box in the attic. My cousin left it last summer. Canvas, brushes, whole nine yards."

I didn't say thank you. I just nodded and let the idea root.

Later that day, I climbed into the attic with a flashlight and a half-dead phone. Dust swirled in the sunbeams like snow. The box was buried under a few crates of holiday stuff and an old typewriter, but it was there—labeled "Art Junk."

I carried it down like it was holy.

That night, while Olivia read a paperback in the chair across the room, I laid everything out on the kitchen table. The brushes were cheap, but they held their shape. The paints were mostly intact, a few tubes dried out at the edges. I picked one—cadmium yellow—and squeezed a line onto the palette. Just that color. That name. It made something hum in my chest.

I didn't know what I was painting. I just started moving.

Long, rough strokes at first. Then smaller ones. Circles, shadows, curves that led nowhere. I wasn't trying to make anything beautiful. I just wanted to see if I could still make.

Olivia didn't interrupt. She just glanced up, smiled once, and went back to her book.

When I stopped, my wrist ached. My fingers were tacky with color. The painting didn't look like much—a blur of yellows and grays and one sharp line of red through the center—but it was mine.

I didn't sleep that night. But not from fear. I stayed up staring at the ceiling, heart still moving like I'd run a mile, thoughts crashing into each other too fast to pin down. But none of it felt like dread.

The next day, I woke up early and ran. Just a mile. Just down the gravel path behind the barn and back. My lungs burned. My legs hated me. But I did it.

He always told me running was a waste. Said, I looked stupid bouncing around like a rabbit. That it made my thighs look too big.

I ran anyway.

I made a playlist that night, too. Music, I hadn't listened to in years. Songs he said were "too much." Ballads that made me cry, punk bands from high school, old country that reminded me of car rides with my dad. I let it blast through Olivia's Bluetooth speaker while I scrubbed the dishes, hair tied up, hips swaying. I sang loud and off-key.

She clapped from the hall. "Hell yes."

Each thing was small. But it felt like gathering the pieces.

That afternoon, we sat on the porch, sipping lemon water from jelly jars. The dog snored at our feet.

"You doing okay?" Olivia asked.

"I don't know what *okay* looks like anymore," I said. "But I think I'm getting closer."

She watched me a minute, then nodded. "You gonna press charges?"

"I don't know yet."

"No rush. Just make sure whatever you do next is for you. Not to make anyone else understand."

"He's gonna spin it," I said. "Make me the crazy one."

"He's already trying. But truth has legs. His stories will fall apart eventually."

I sat with that. Let it settle.

"Thank you," I said finally.

"You're not thanking me for shit. You did this. I just held the door open."

I laughed, wiped my eyes.

Later that week, I painted again. Then again. I started sketching during breakfast, scribbling notes in the margins of old grocery lists. I ran a little farther each day. I emailed my sister from a new address, just a photo of the pasture and the line: I'm okay. I'm somewhere safe. I'll explain soon.

I didn't get a reply right away, but I sent another one a few days later.

Each time I opened my sketchbook, I filled more of it.

Each time the phone buzzed, it wasn't him.

Each breath I took didn't belong to anyone else anymore.

Unmasking the Truth

THE BUILDING DIDN'T LOOK like much—just an old tan brick office between a dentist and a UPS store, with a tiny hand-painted sign that read "Stillwater Therapy." Olivia drove me the first time, she waited in the parking lot with a thermos of coffee and her dog curled up in the backseat. I hadn't argued. My stomach had been too tight to speak.

The waiting room smelled like lavender and printer ink. There was a stack of magazines nobody read and a fake plant that needed dusting. A receptionist with kind eyes handed me a clipboard and said softly, "Take your time."

I didn't take my time. I rushed through the forms like they were a test, barely breathing. Name. Birthdate. Emergency contact. Have you experienced trauma? Do you feel safe now?

I checked the boxes. Yes. No. Sometimes.

When they called my name, I stood too fast and knocked my knee against the corner of the table. It hurt, but I barely noticed.

The therapist was maybe in her forties, sharp-eyed but soft-spoken. She introduced herself—I forget her last name now, just remember she told me to call her Cam. Her office was small, just a couch and two chairs, a lamp with warm light, a basket of tissues beside the coffee table. There was a bookshelf behind her, loaded with paperbacks and a single worn teddy bear tucked between the spines.

She let me sit wherever I wanted. I chose the chair closest to the door.

We started slow. She asked about me, not Austin. Where I was from. What I used to like. How long I'd been gone. I gave short answers, eyes on my chipped nails. I don't remember most of that session. I just remember how quiet she was. How she didn't rush to fill the silence. How she didn't flinch when I said, I left him but hadn't told anyone but two people.

When I said, "It's complicated," she nodded. When I said, "He's not a monster, he just... wasn't always like this," she said nothing for a long time. Then she asked, "Can I share something?"

I nodded.

She leaned forward, elbows on her knees, and said, "It's okay to still love someone who hurt you. It doesn't mean it wasn't abuse."

I stared at her.

She had said it. The word.

I didn't cry. My spine locked up like it was bracing for a blow. My throat felt like I'd swallowed gravel. I wanted to correct her, wanted to say, "No, it wasn't like that." But I didn't. Because it *was* like that.

I left that first session with a migraine and a paper in my purse she'd handed me at the end— "Common Responses to Psychological Abuse." I read it in the passenger seat on the way home while Olivia hummed along to the radio. Every bullet point felt like a punch.

Guilt. Hypervigilance. Loss of identity. Difficulty trusting. Feeling crazy. Isolating from loved ones. Confusion. Numbness. Obsessive thoughts.

I folded the paper twice before I shoved it under the seat.

The next few appointments were messier. I fumbled through the words like my mouth wasn't made for them. My tongue tripped over "manipulate" and "control" like I was still protecting him. I said things like, "He didn't mean to," and "It only happened once like that," and "I could've tried harder to..."

Cam cut me off then, not unkindly.

"That's not your job," she said.

I stared at my lap.

She waited until I looked up again. "It's not your job to manage his anger. Or make him gentle. Or explain away bruises."

I swallowed hard. My hands curled into fists in my lap.

That day I told her about the wrist.

About the glass of tea, I hadn't rinsed right. The way he'd grabbed my arm and yanked so fast I hadn't registered the pain until hours later. The purple blooming up my shoulder. How he'd kissed my temple right after and told me to relax.

Cam asked how I felt when I remembered it.

I said, "Like it happened to someone else."

She nodded. "That's a trauma response."

The way she said it—calm, steady, like naming something didn't make it grow fangs—made me breathe deeper.

We didn't just talk about him. She asked about my art. I told her I used to paint. Used to sketch in class, napkins, the corners of grocery lists. I told her about the new canvas in Olivia's kitchen and how my hands didn't shake when I picked up the brush.

"That's your voice," she said. "It's coming back."

I almost smiled.

We talked about my sister, too. Lemon. How I'd drifted from her slowly, like being led into a fog I didn't notice until

I couldn't find the shore. I told Cam how he'd always made snide comments when I said her name. Called her dramatic. Said she filled my head with bullshit. How eventually I'd stopped calling because it felt easier.

"Isolation isn't always obvious," Cam said. "It's not about locking the door—it's about convincing you the door isn't there."

The next week, I wrote Lemon a letter.

I didn't send it. Just wrote it. Four pages. Front and back. I didn't apologize. I just told the truth. About how I disappeared without meaning to. How I thought I had to stay small to be safe. How I was trying to be something better now.

Cam told me later that was progress. "You're reclaiming narrative."

Another phrase I wrote down in my journal and stared at, until it didn't look like English anymore.

The hardest part was talking about the good memories. Because they made me feel crazy. How he used to tuck my hair behind my ear, or leave sticky notes on the fridge that said things like "You're mine, Sunshine." Cam said, abusers often alternate kindness and cruelty to confuse you, to hook you.

"He gave you breadcrumbs so you wouldn't notice you were starving," she said.

That one landed deep.

I started bringing my sketchbook to sessions. Not to show her. Just to hold. It helped me feel real. One week, I drew a horse the way I used to at Rustlers Ridge, lines soft around the legs, harsh at the mouth. She pointed to the eyes and said, "That's how you looked the first day."

I didn't know what to say.

So, I drew more.

Outside of therapy, I started speaking up. Just in small ways. I corrected Olivia when she misremembered something from high school. I told a guy at the gas station; I didn't need help pumping. I posted a photo of the pasture on a new account. No caption. Just light.

The phone didn't buzz.

The next session, I talked about the dreams. Not the nightmares—those were familiar. But the new ones. Where I was driving a truck across a wide-open field. Where I had no destination but didn't feel lost. Where I wasn't hiding.

Cam smiled when I said that. "That's your mind practicing safety."

I bit my lip to keep from crying.

At the end of the sixth session, she said, "You're not broken. You adapted—and now you're undoing that adaptation."

I didn't nod. I just held the words like they were something delicate and alive.

Back at Olivia's, I painted a new canvas. Yellow sweeping upward, rust-red beneath. A figure small in the distance, arms wide, mouth open.

Not screaming. Singing.

The Yellow Revival

THE CARDIGAN WAS SOFT and worn at the elbows—the kind of yellow that reminded me of lemonade, and August, and porch lights left on too long. It hung on the rack between a churchy floral blouse and a denim jacket with a busted zipper. I don't know what made me reach for it—maybe the color, maybe the price tag, maybe just the fact I could. I hadn't worn anything like it in years. Not since before he started making jokes about how yellow made me look "washed out," like I was trying too hard. I'd stopped wearing it after that. Stopped buying anything bright at all.

I pulled it from the hanger and held it up to my chest. It didn't match anything I owned. That made me want it more.

The thrift store was quiet, except for the hum of the fluorescent lights and the occasional squeak of hangers being shuffled on the rack behind me. Olivia waited at the register, flipping through a stack of used vinyl with one hand and sipping a gas station soda with the other. I didn't ask if I should get the cardigan. I just walked over and tossed it on top of her stack.

She looked up, raised an eyebrow, then smiled. "Look at you."

"Don't," I muttered, but I smiled, too.

Later that week, I bought a yellow journal from the corner drugstore. I didn't even mean to. I'd walked in for toothpaste and left with it tucked under my arm, like it belonged there. The cover had a tiny sun pressed into the leather, so faint you had to tilt it toward the light to see it. I carried it around for days before I wrote in it.

The first page I didn't date. Just scribbled half a sentence, crossed it out, then wrote: I don't know who I am without him.

I left it there. Closed the cover. Put it back on the shelf next to my bed.

The mug came next. Pale yellow, chipped on the rim, with "HELLO SUNSHINE" painted across the front in curling letters. I found it at a garage sale down the road from Olivia's. A teenage girl manning the cash box smiled as I handed her a dollar and said, "That was my mom's favorite."

I said, "I think it's mine now."

The girl grinned. "Good. I like when things get second chances."

That one stayed with me.

Olivia didn't say anything when the guest room started changing. I tucked the cardigan over the back of the rocking chair in the corner. Set the journal on the nightstand beside a cracked ceramic bowl I found in the kitchen, which I filled with tiny stones from the pasture. I added the mug last, placed it on the windowsill where it caught the morning light.

Eventually, she noticed. Or maybe she always had. She walked in one afternoon carrying clean sheets and paused at the door.

"You're nesting," she said.

"Is that a problem?"

"Nope." She set the sheets down and started stripping the bed. "You were always the one who made things look better. Remember that?"

I didn't. Not really. But I liked the idea of it.

Music crept back in after that. I started playing playlists on her old Bluetooth speaker while I made coffee, folded laundry, or cleaned out the tack room. Not sad songs. Not angry ones, either. Just soft things—golden strings, easy vocals, and the occasional piano that made the back of my throat sting. I hummed along without realizing, sang under my breath when I thought I was alone.

One morning, Olivia caught me swaying by the kitchen sink, barefoot, rinsing dishes while some indie folk band played through the speaker. She didn't say anything. Just raised her coffee in salute as she passed by with a smirk.

I let the music keep playing.

The world didn't shift all at once. There were still nights I bolted upright in bed, half-convinced I'd heard his truck in the driveway. Still days where I flinched when the landline rang, or froze at the sight of a tall man in a ball cap at the feed store. Still dreams I woke from with sweat pooling at my collarbone, my hands clenched around the bedsheets like rope.

But those moments got smaller. Not easier—but smaller. Less loud.

The mornings helped. I started getting up early again, even before Olivia. I'd sneak outside with a blanket draped across my shoulders to sit on the porch swing, knees curled to my chest, mug in hand. The sky was widest then. Soft blues melting into orange, like the world was remembering how to wake up. I let it teach me.

One of those mornings, I opened the yellow journal again.

This time, I wrote without crossing anything out.

I miss who I was before I started asking permission to breathe. I miss laughing without checking the room. I miss my sister. I miss feeling safe in my own skin. I'm learning how to come back.

The pen shook as I put it down.

That day, I painted. Not just little things, not just strokes on the edge of my sketchbook. I pulled out the canvas I'd been avoiding, and set it up on the back deck. Olivia left me alone, only sticking her head out once to ask if I needed more water.

The colors weren't planned. Yellow, sure—layers of it. But I added streaks of crimson, too. Lines of moss, teal, and even black—sharp across the corners. It wasn't pretty. Not in a traditional sense. It was raw, crooked, and bleeding at the edges.

I loved it.

At dinner, I showed Olivia. She studied it for a long time, longer than I expected, then said, "This feels like you."

"It doesn't make any sense."

"Neither did what you went through. Doesn't mean it's not real."

We ate spaghetti on the back porch, feet kicked up on a cooler, music playing low, stars just starting to bleed through the dark.

Later, she handed me a second plate of garlic bread and said, "You don't have to rush any of this."

"I know."

"Good." She glanced at the painting, then back at me. "But you're doing it."

I didn't say anything. Just took the bread and looked out at the pasture.

Fireflies flickered low in the grass, slow and silent.

That night I stayed up journaling. Pages and pages. I wrote down things he used to say. The lies I'd swallowed. The way my own voice had shrunk to match his. I wrote about the first time I thought about leaving, and the way he'd cried when I confronted him, promised to do better, kissed my forehead like I was breakable.

I wrote about how I stayed.

How I stayed again.

And again.

Then I wrote: I'm not staying anymore.

The ink smudged from my hand. I left it.

The next morning, I found a box on the kitchen table. Olivia had labeled it "Sunshine Shit" in sharpie. Inside was a bag of yellow pencils, a scarf, a notepad shaped like a lemon, a small jar of marigold honey, and a print of a sunrise with a horse in the distance.

I blinked hard.

She walked in, carrying a mug of her own and said, "Couldn't help myself."

I grinned and hugged her. Tight.

When I pulled away, she said, "You're gonna be okay, you know."

"I'm starting to believe that."

"Good. Because you've got a whole lotta living left to do."

We laughed and stood there for a while, coffee cooling between us, the box between our hands.

And for the first time in a very long time, I didn't feel like I had to look behind me.

I let the light come in.

The drive back from Salt Lake started quiet, the kind of tired silence that happens after a long day where nothing goes wrong, but everything takes just a little more effort than you expected. I sat with one leg tucked beneath me, picking at the cracked edge of a to-go cup sleeve—cardboard peeling under my thumb. Olivia hummed along to a song on the radio, something twangy and old that reminded me of Sunday mornings when her mother still sang through the kitchen window.

We'd hit a couple thrift shops, stopped for lunch at a taco stand with folding chairs and no posted menu, then wandered around a plant nursery where I'd almost talked myself into buying a snake plant. I'd left it behind, told myself I didn't need one more thing to take care of. Olivia said, "Maybe next time," and I nodded like I believed in that.

The sun hung low by the time we crested the last rise into Grantsville. From the highway, I could just make out the lines of Olivia's property—the wooden posts lining the pasture, the wind-battered mailbox with the tilted red flag, the weathered barn with its leaning door like it had one hip cocked in protest. It always looked like home, even though I still didn't know what that word meant for me.

Then I saw it.

My breath snagged halfway up my throat and never finish the climb.

The yellow Jeep sat at the edge of the driveway like a wound. Or a threat. Bent front bumper folded like paper. The windshield caved in, spiderwebbed glass catching the last of the sun. One of the tires completely shredded. My old air freshener—the little wooden honeybee—still dangled from the rearview mirror, twisted sideways. Like it was mocking me.

I didn't remember unbuckling. I just knew my door was open and my boots hit gravel before Olivia had even put the truck in park.

She was right behind me, voice sharp. "What the hell—"

"It's mine," I said, almost tripping on the uneven stones as I rushed toward it. "That's my Jeep."

I stopped just short of it, chest heaving, palms open at my sides like I needed the air to touch them before I could be sure this was real. I'd left it behind, hadn't I? Parked it at the house I'd escaped from. Not even locked. I'd told myself it didn't matter, because it wasn't legally mine. His name was on the paperwork. He'd made sure of that.

Olivia circled around the front, crouched low to inspect the tire. "Someone dropped it here like they were delivering fucking groceries."

I wanted to laugh. Or throw up. I wasn't sure which.

A wind picked up across the pasture and caught the edge of the passenger door—it creaked open, then slammed shut again. The sound cracked through my ribs.

"It's a message."

I said it like a fact, not a question. Because it was.

She stood, dusted her hands on her jeans. "You're calling the cops."

My mouth opened, then closed. My skin buzzed with heat, my heart a stuttered warning drum in my chest. I hated how fast the fear returned, how it tucked itself under my tongue like it belonged there.

"He didn't touch me," I said, barely above a whisper. "Technically—"

"Fuck technically." Olivia's voice was steel. "He brought this here. Totaled your car and parked it on my land. He doesn't get to do that."

My legs were jelly, my vision too sharp. I reached for my phone, fingers fumbling. I'd underestimated how deep he was willing to go.

I didn't even want the Jeep. I just wanted the message erased.

I punched in the non-emergency line. Gave my name. My voice barely cracked when I said, "I think I need to file a report."

They dispatched someone. Twenty minutes.

I stood with my arms wrapped tight around myself, eyes fixed on the ruin of yellow metal like if I blinked, it would vanish. Olivia paced behind me, muttering under her breath, hands clenched into fists at her sides. I couldn't stop picturing his face. The smug satisfaction he probably wore as he walked away. Maybe he even laughed.

He used to say, I was lucky. That anyone else would've thrown me out. That he put up with me. That he gave me more than I deserved.

"You okay?" Olivia asked, stepping closer.

"No."

It felt good to say it. Awful, but good.

When the cop car finally pulled up—lights off, but that slow rolling crawl that told you they were reading the situation—I stepped forward, arms still crossed. I explained everything. That I'd left. That the Jeep wasn't mine anymore, but it used to be. That he'd dropped it here as a message. That he didn't say anything, not directly, but I didn't need words to understand this. He was trying to scare me. Remind me who still held the strings.

The deputy asked questions, nodded a lot, took photos. I gave him Austin's name. Explained the history without giving the whole war. Mentioned the protection order I hadn't filed for yet. The bruises I hadn't documented. The silence I'd lived in for too long.

He said he'd file the report. That technically, the car wasn't stolen. That if I wanted to press charges for harassment or intimidation, I'd need to start documenting. Paper trails. Texts. Calls. Photos. Screenshots.

I wanted to scream. To throw the Jeep into a canyon. To light the damn thing on fire and dance around it like a funeral pyre.

When the deputy left, I stood staring at the Jeep again.

"You okay?" Olivia asked again, more cautious this time.

I shook my head. "No. I'm pissed."

"Good."

She pulled her phone out of her pocket, snapped a photo of the Jeep. "We're keeping records now. He wants to play games? Fine. Let's play smarter."

I looked at the broken glass, the way the sun hit it just right and made the cracks shimmer like a spiderweb. It was awful. But it was also, just a car. A fucked-up machine. Not a part of me. Not anymore.

That night, I sat at Olivia's kitchen table with a glass of wine and a notepad. Started a new list. Not the one of things he took—but one of things I was building back. Trust. Sanity. Control. The right to drink wine without flinching. The right to wear yellow. The right to exist without explanation.

When Olivia sat down across from me, I showed her the list. She added something in her own messy scrawl: **Power**.

"Don't forget," she said. "You've got it."

I didn't answer. Just stared at the word.

The next morning, the Jeep was gone. Towed by a guy Olivia knew from high school. No ceremony. Just a rumble, a winch, and a trail of oil on the gravel. Watching it disappear was like pulling out a rotten tooth—painful, but necessary.

After it was gone, I stood in the driveway, toes digging into the dirt, and breathed deep.

I wasn't scared of him. Not in the same way.

He could send all the messages he wanted.

I wasn't opening them anymore.

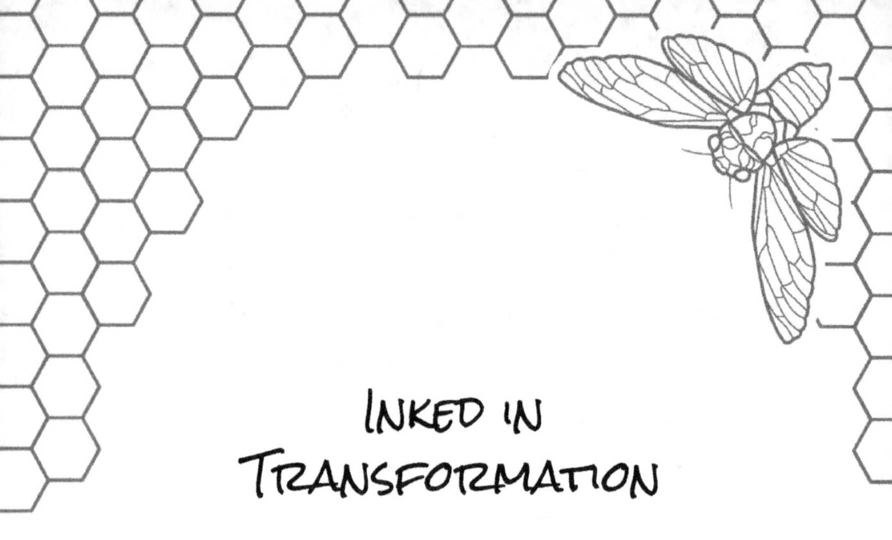

Inked in Transformation

I walked into the tattoo parlor and fought the instinct to bolt back out the door. The place was loud. Plexiglass cases held shiny designs in sterile light. The hum of the machines mingled with radio music I couldn't place, everyone talking about weekend plans or lunch specials, like it was a normal day. It felt wrong for my quiet world.

Still. I'd saved for this specifically. I had that list taped up in my notebook—small steps in reclaiming myself—and getting a tattoo was step forty-two, or maybe fifty-two, or maybe it was the final. A cicada, perched where the bony dip of my arm shows when I raise it.

I pulled off the cardigan I wore—lemon yellow now stained with dirt and coffee. I rolled up my sleeve—looked at the blank skin, pale with early sun freckles I used to think were strange. They were mine. I traced the shape of my wrist. Olivia squeezed my hand.

"You're allowed to do this," she said softly. Unformed smiles danced behind her green eyes.

I wanted to shake, hell yes. Instead, I huffed out a breath. "No backing out."

The artist, a wiry guy with inked-up fingers, nodded. I felt his breath warm on the back of my neck when he leaned over to check the placement. I flinched like it meant something.

"It's good," he said. "Want me to start?"

Olivia squeezed again. I set my jaw and nodded.

The first buzz startled me, loud, gritty, not violent, just business. I sucked air in and tightened in the chair. My arm trembled. The needle pressed in—pain sharp, and surprising but bearable. I stared at the ceiling, traced the light fixture. A cicada wing sprouted tiny lines, arcs of black ink. My breath steadied.

Olivia hummed a tune I remembered from my high school playlist—something silly—but it felt like tethering to simpler days.

"How's it feel?" she asked, when the line elongated behind the artist's hand.

"Vibrates," I said. Not what I expected, but not scary either. Felt like waking up cold.

The cicada body took shape: oval, symmetrical, wings veined like cathedral glass. I watched as it was drawn into me as the buzzing machine gnawed at the skin. I tried to track what parts hurt—nothing major, just persistent, a reminder this was real. Ink was permanent.

Inside, my pulse thudded. I thought of all the damage I'd let in. The bruises he denied. The water splashed on glass I didn't rinse fast enough. The phone calls I deleted and never made. The years of quiet triumphs erased by his voice saying I was too—too loud, too emotional, too broken.

Too much.

The cicada marked a boundary. No more silence.

When he wiped off the ink from the stencil and pressed the needle in again, I breathed slow. When he dove into the wings, detailed and fine, I closed my eyes and felt my scalp tingle—not fear but something braced for a shift.

Olivia stayed beside me, hand in mine. Someone walked by with old-school emo song on their earbuds. The parlor chair rattled. A laugh behind me. Life, strange and noisy.

I let the buzzing become background noise. I slid between repurposed pain and promise.

When it finished, the cicada looked done—black and crisp and more revealing than I expected. The skin around it was red, swollen, it pulsed warm. I ran my other hand over it; fingers slick with ointment.

"There she is," Olivia said, voice soft and proud. She reached out and tapped the ink then looked me in the eyes. "That's your signal."

I nodded, and touched the design again. The lines were etched, real. I let tears come—quiet, mild, honest. I'd worried I wouldn't feel anything. Instead, I felt everything.

I pulled down my sleeve again and stepped out of the chair. My heart felt balanced between something small and something fierce.

We paid, room echoing coins and printers. On the way home, the valley sank gold beneath the dusky sky. I drove slower than usual, left the amber-colored parking lights on as we rolled through Grantsville into the pasture drive.

Back at the barn, I got out of the truck barefoot then slid a smock over my cardigan and went looking for paint again. The yellow sweater wasn't clean anymore. I smiled. It wasn't meant to stay pristine.

I reached to wipe mud off the wall beside the studio door and stalled—saw the cicada when my sleeve slipped. My fingers touched the swelled skin. I didn't wince.

Inside, I pulled out the big canvas I'd started months ago. The one with streaks of crimson across amber. I added lines for wings, arcs that mirrored the cicada shape. I dragged yellow atop red to soften it. Paint splashed off the brush onto my cardigan. I didn't care.

Olivia came to the open studio door. "That's perfect," she said.

I didn't argue. I picked up another brush. Painted wing veins over the horizon shape. Dripped ink along the edges.

I painted until my fingers bled color. Until the studio smelled warm and thick with drying paint.

When I finally pulled the smock off, I traced my veins running golden across chest, arms, hands. The cicada shimmered bright under sunlight.

Songs drifted in from the house. Faint laughter. She was making tea.

I leaned there, pressed brush handle in my palm. I breathed easy enough to feel curious again. I hadn't smiled all day. Not even then, not until I looked at the painting and saw wings spread across yellow fields. Then I whispered softly to the canvas: *fly again.*

When I sat on the porch a few hours later, the evening sky washed pink across the pasture, I felt the buzz of the cicada skin under my cardigan. That buzzing meant I survived. I was alive. I would last.

I turned my wrist in front of the window, stared at the design shimmering in the growing dusk. Not scarred. Not hidden. Not ashamed. Just ink breathing light.

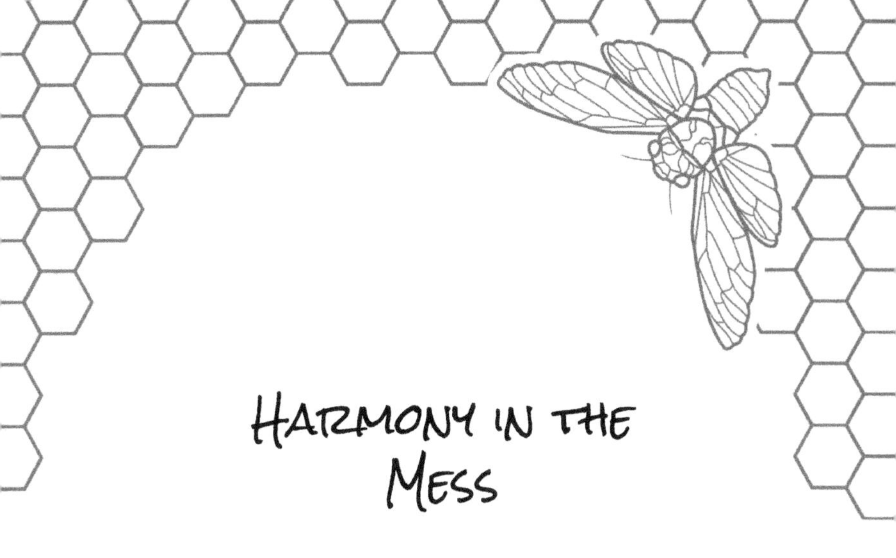

Harmony in the Mess

I USED TO HATE my own logo. Funny how something I designed with so much pride could start to look like a joke after *he* ripped it apart enough times. He said it was too soft, too feminine, too amateur. "No one's gonna take you seriously with that watercolor bird-shit," he'd muttered once, slamming his beer on the counter like it was the period at the end of a sentence I wasn't allowed to argue with.

Now the faded original sketch sat pinned to the wall beside Olivia's kitchen table, curled at the edges from being rolled in a storage box too long. It was still mine. Still soft. Still watercolor. I didn't touch it up. I didn't sharpen the edges. I left the imperfect H looping into the stem of a branch because I remembered the exact afternoon I made it—sunlight through the studio window, my coffee cold because I forgot it existed.

Haven and Harmony Interiors. I typed the name again into a blank Instagram bio and hit save before I could talk myself out of it. The screen blinked. My hands were already sweating. I took another sip of iced tea, citrus and cold, and wiped my palms on my jeans.

"I made it live," I said aloud, not even realizing I'd spoken until Olivia called from the next room.

"Good. Want me to make the first fake order?"

I laughed, the sound coming out sharp and surprised. "Please don't. My confidence is hanging on by, like, two threads and a safety pin."

"Then it's stronger than duct tape, babe. You're good."

I stared at the page. No followers. No posts. A blank canvas in a world already saturated with perfection. I didn't know what the hell I was doing. I didn't know if clients would trust someone who ghosted for years, only to resurface with a trauma-flavored backstory and a Pinterest board full of moody blues and warm neutrals. But I wanted this. My fingers reached for my sketchpad, flipping it open to where I'd doodled shelving ideas and color palettes in between therapy notes and tear stains.

I posted the first photo without a caption—a sunlit corner of Olivia's guest room, the one I'd slowly transformed with thrifted art and a throw pillow I made out of an old curtain.

The light caught the yellow cardigan I'd draped across the chair, not on purpose, but it stayed in the shot anyway.

My phone vibrated two minutes later. A follow. Then another.

"You gonna watch the notifications all day or actually send out emails like you said you would?" Olivia said, stepping into the kitchen and grabbing a plum from the bowl between us.

"I'm working on it," I mumbled, dragging my laptop closer. I'd written five draft messages to old clients—safe ones, the kind who wouldn't press for explanations—and I reread them all for the sixth time before hitting send.

An hour later, my e-mail pinged.

Available for a consultation next week?

I covered my mouth with my hand and just sat there. I wanted to scream. Or cry. Or bolt into the backyard and run laps around the pasture like a golden retriever.

Instead, I typed: Yes, I'd love to. Let's talk.

The reply came back fast. Like someone had been waiting. I ran my fingers over the keyboard, then over the wooden grain of the table, then over my own arm—over the cicada tattoo, still healing, still warm when I pressed it too hard. I breathed through the rush of adrenaline, the tangled joy, nerves and lingering shadow of a man who would hate every second of this, if he knew.

I closed the laptop and looked at Olivia. She was peeling the plum with her thumbnail, teeth working on a sunflower seed.

"Can I borrow your truck next Tuesday?"

She nodded without looking up. "Course. Just don't wreck it like your Jeep."

"Too soon."

"Never too soon. Proud of you, by the way."

I stood up to grab another tea, feeling like I needed to move or I'd start shaking. "It's just one client."

"It's not. It's a stake in the ground. You put your name out there again. That's not nothing."

I didn't answer. I just leaned against the fridge and let the cool air roll out across my bare arms while the ice maker groaned in its usual tired way. I held the cold tea bottle against my cheek.

Later that afternoon, I sat cross-legged on the floor of the guest room with fabric swatches spread around me like autumn leaves. I ran my hands over each texture—linen, cotton, velvet. I closed my eyes and remembered the rush of pulling together a space. The way it felt to walk into a blank room and start imagining who would live there, breathe there, laugh there. I used to be good at this.

I picked up my sketchpad again and started drawing. A dining room built around light. A reading nook with a crescent-shaped chair. I added notes in the margins, scribbled arrows. By the time the sun began dipping over the fields, I'd filled three pages.

Dinner was leftover pasta and quiet TV. Olivia passed me a bowl and sat beside me on the couch like she had every evening for the last few weeks, both of us finding our own rituals without asking. Her dog snored from beneath the coffee table. I felt my phone buzz again, checked it, expecting another weird spam follow.

But it was someone I hadn't heard from in three years. A former client, someone who used to refer to me as "magic with light and space." The message said: Heard you're designing again. You available?

I showed Olivia. She raised both eyebrows. "You need a website yet, or you gonna wait till five more of those show up?"

I bit into a forkful of pasta and mumbled around it, "Website it is."

The next few days were a blur of tasks. I built the website with a template and sheer willpower, uploaded old projects I managed to recover from a thumb drive I'd nearly tossed out. I emailed more people. I ran errands. I set up a second bank account. I watched YouTube videos on how to handle freelance taxes and sobbed once—hard, because it all felt too big.

But I didn't quit.

The first consultation happened in a bakery. I wore jeans and a flowy blouse, nothing fancy, but it was the first time in months I'd picked an outfit because I liked how it looked—not how it made me disappear. The client was kind. She asked questions. She signed a contract. I walked out with a deposit check burning a hole in my pocket and called Olivia before I'd even reached the truck.

She answered on the first ring. "So?"

"I got it."

She whooped so loud I had to hold the phone away from my ear.

That night, I curled up on the porch wrapped in an old quilt. The cicadas hummed somewhere in the grass, invisible but relentless. I traced the tattoo again as I watched the stars blink to life.

I was working again. Really working. Not just to survive. Not to placate. Not to maintain someone else's story about who I was, or what I should be. This was mine. Every messy email, every brush of fabric, every line I drew and plan I made—was building something.

The fear didn't vanish. It still sat nearby, especially when I saw a black truck that looked too familiar or heard a song that yanked me back. But now it didn't steer the wheel. I did.

And somewhere deep in the part of me that hadn't dared believe in second chances, I knew I'd never give this up again. Not for anyone. Not for anything.

The third time I slipped a rug into the back of the truck, my elbow clipped the tailgate and I swore so loud the rooster out by the barn let out a squawk in protest.

From the driver's side, Olivia snorted. "That rug giving you attitude again?"

I rubbed the sore spot and shoved the corner down harder. "It thinks it's in charge."

"Good luck with that," she said, hopping down from the cab. She tugged the door shut with her boot and walked over, a plastic grocery sack dangling from one hand. "I brought the good trail mix this time. No raisins."

"You're a hero."

"I know."

We loaded the rest of the staging stuff in silence—lamps, a woven basket full of throw pillows, a delicate chair with a leg I'd glued back together that morning like a surgeon setting a bone. The truck smelled like furniture polish and lavender from one of the sachets Olivia stuffed in every pocket she could find. I sank into the passenger seat and took the trail mix. She handed me the bag with a grin, then reached to start the truck. The engine groaned before settling into its usual low hum.

We'd done this enough times now, we didn't need to map it out. I handled the front room; she tackled anything that needed lifting or ladder work. She refused to let me climb anything higher than a stool after the bookshelf incident, which we still don't talk about because I still swore that plank was steady. It wasn't.

The house today was a modest ranch-style near the foothills, wide porch, decent bones, outdated everything. A young couple inherited it from someone's aunt and wanted it "modern but cozy" and "Instagrammable without being obvious." I'd nodded and said yes to all of it, because I understood what it meant even if they didn't know how to phrase it. People wanted comfort without admitting how badly they needed it.

The front door creaked. Olivia hauled the bench to the entryway while I set the rug, then unrolled fabric swatches across the floor to match the accent chairs I'd brought.

"You like the blue or the ochre?" I held them up side by side.

She pointed with her chin. "Blue. It softens the tile."

I nodded. "You're getting good at this."

"I know," she said again, grinning. "Do I get a cut of your first million?"

"You'll get a sandwich and the last of my sparkling water. That's the budget."

The next hour passed in color. A gallery wall with reclaimed wood frames. The way sunlight bounced off the gold trim of the mirror I nearly didn't bring. Throw blankets folded into triangles, cushions fluffed like clouds. I didn't talk much. I got like that when I worked—sharp, fast, focused—but Olivia never took it personally. She handed me a protein bar at one point; I barely registered it until I'd already eaten half of it.

The couple showed up near the end. They were polite, surprised, overjoyed, one of them nearly cried, which made me shift awkwardly and pretend I needed to wipe down a table leg. After they left, I slumped against the truck bed and tilted my head to the sky.

"I need a goddamn nap."

"No naps until you come back inside and look at your email," Olivia said, nudging my ankle with her foot. "You got another inquiry. New one. Some café wants you to design a patio space."

My eyes fluttered open. "Wait, seriously?"

"Yup. Just came through. And your post with the yellow throw got shared by some local design page. People are paying attention."

I stared at her. "That's... wild."

"It's not. It's earned."

The sun was starting to drop low again, the light turning golden and heavy across the hills. I climbed into the truck without answering, too wrung out to know what I wanted to say. She didn't push.

Back at the ranch, I showered off the day—sweat, dust, a few paint flecks I hadn't noticed—and pulled on a sweatshirt that still smelled like Olivia's detergent. I wandered into the kitchen barefoot, the floor cool under my toes, and watched her slice up fruit like we were at summer camp.

"Your knee okay?" she asked, nodding toward where I'd been limping a little earlier.

"Yeah. Just banged it climbing out the window during staging."

"You what?"

"Don't worry about it."

She shook her head but didn't scold me. Just handed over a bowl of melon and plopped down on the opposite stool. I sat too, curling my legs underneath me, and opened my laptop.

The email was real. So was another one, tucked just below it. And a DM from someone asking if I did gift certificates for staging. I blinked at the screen, not sure how to absorb any of it.

I used to daydream about being this busy. Then I stopped letting myself. Then I forgot how to even imagine it.

"I think I'm gonna need a calendar," I muttered.

"You need an assistant."

"Too soon."

"You'll see."

I chewed on a piece of cantaloupe and looked around the room. I'd started rearranging things in the guest house too—small touches, just enough to feel like I was leaving fingerprints on the world again. The gold-framed mirror by the door. The cluster of pressed flower prints. The yellow mug I never let anyone else use.

I didn't call it healing. That word made it sound like there was an endpoint. But I was moving. I was building. I was filling spaces with softness, instead of silence. Each room I touched, each project I finished, was a kind of answer to a question I hadn't dared ask for years.

Was I still in there?

The one who used to dream in floor plans and color gradients. The one who believed light mattered. Who trusted her own eye. Who used to sing in her car and stop at every estate sale on a whim.

She was harder to find than I expected. But she wasn't gone.

Later that night, after Olivia had gone to bed and the house was dim except for the porch light humming outside, I walked out to the barn. The air was cooler, the sky stretched wide and was freckled with stars. The goats were asleep, one of the barn cats watched me from the top rail, like I was interrupting her peace.

I leaned on the fence and breathed deep.

I didn't have to apologize for being tired. I didn't owe anyone quiet obedience. I didn't have to shrink. I didn't have to soften the word abuse just because it made other people uncomfortable. I didn't have to dress like someone else's idea of respectable.

And I didn't have to stop at survival.

The fence creaked beneath my arms. The breeze tugged at the hem of my sweatshirt. I stood there for a long time before I finally turned back toward the house. The porch light buzzed, casting a soft glow onto the grass. Inside, my sketchpad waited, open to a new page.

I wasn't done. Not even close.

Lemon and Honey

THE SKY WAS A smeared a watercolor of dusty pinks and low tired-grays when Lemon pulled the truck off the gravel road and killed the engine. The foothills curled around us like they were trying to hold something steady, and maybe that's why we came here. Or maybe she just knew I'd need open air and quiet before I could say any of it.

She climbed into the truck bed without a word, tossing a wool blanket over the tailgate like we were just kids again, sneaking sodas and jokes after chores. I followed; coffee mug pressed to my palms. The thermos still steamed when I handed it back, and she refilled my cup without asking if I wanted more.

We didn't talk at first. It was the kind of quiet that usually made me itch—made me check my phone, shift in my seat, smooth my shirt like I was being watched. But I didn't reach for anything this time. I just let the silence stretch, watching how the sky softened at the edges and the mountains caught the last warmth of the sun.

She took a sip and let out a small sigh. "Remember when we tried to dig a pool over that way?" She pointed down the slope near a thicket of chokecherry trees.

I let out a dry laugh. "Yeah. We got through, what, five inches of clay before we hit roots and gave up?"

"You cried because you thought that meant we'd have to live the rest of our lives without a pool. I told you we could just fill the hole with water and sit in it."

"I actually did." The corners of my mouth twitched. "I came back out the next day with a bucket and tried."

She chuckled low and warm. "You had stubborn down to a science."

That hung in the air between us, rolling around until it made something sharp in me twitch. I looked down into my cup, watching the way the heat curled upward. My fingers curled around it tighter. "He hated that about me."

Lennon didn't answer. Not with words. She angled her body slightly, enough to face me but not enough to make me feel cornered.

"He called it defiance." My voice cracked. I hated how it cracked. "Said, it was disrespect. Said, I didn't know how to be grateful."

"You don't owe me an explanation," she said quietly. "But I'm here. All the way."

I nodded, staring at the curve of her boot where it tapped against the side of the truck bed. My stomach twisted so tightly, I felt like I'd choke on my next breath. "He didn't start by yelling. That came later. First it was little things. Questions that sounded like concern. 'Do you *really* want to wear that?' 'Is she *really* your friend?' 'Why didn't you call me right away?' Like he was just trying to take care of me."

Her jaw tensed, but she stayed silent.

"Then it got louder. Harder. Suddenly, I was always doing something wrong. He didn't like how I arranged the silverware, how I parked, how I spoke to the guy at the drive-thru. It was like... like he was always measuring me against this ruler I didn't even know existed."

She reached over, slow and steady, and set her hand over mine.

"I stopped calling," I said, barely above a whisper. "Stopped visiting. I told myself it was because I was busy, because life gets like that, but really? I was scared he'd find out. Or worse—that he'd come with me. And everyone would see what he was really like."

"He's not your shame to carry."

I bit the inside of my cheek until it hurt. "He would grab my arm. Not all the time. But enough. And he'd say I was imagining it when I said he hurt me. One time, he threw my keys into the sink and said I was too emotional to drive. Said, I'd probably crash on purpose just to make him look bad. I started hiding my money in the lining of my coat. I memorized the sound of his footsteps when he was angry."

Lemon's face didn't twist or flinch. She didn't say sorry, or ask why I didn't tell her sooner. She just listened, eyes steady and full of something that wasn't pity—it was fury, disguised as love.

"He showed up at Olivia's last month. Tracked my phone. Brought my old Jeep. He wrecked it and dumped it in the driveway."

"Jesus."

"I filed a report. Changed my number again. Got everything locked down tight. But I still wake up like I'm going to find him standing over me."

"You won't," she said flatly. "And if he tries, he'll have to get through a whole damn wall of us."

I nodded. I couldn't say thank you. It didn't feel like enough.

The breeze picked up, tossing strands of my hair into my mouth. I didn't bother brushing them away. I leaned back on my palms and stared up at the sky, tracing a crooked line across the clouds. "I got a tattoo."

She snorted. "You did not."

"Little cicada. On my arm. It still stings."

"That's metal as hell."

"I wanted something that reminded me, I'm still alive. Still here."

"Well, you picked the right bug. Loud little bastards that dig their way out after years in the dirt."

I laughed so hard I almost spilled my coffee. "I didn't think of it like that."

She nudged my boot with hers. "You always wanted to fly. You used to make wings out of chicken wire and duct tape."

"They never worked."

"No, but you never stopped trying."

I let my eyes close, soaking in the way the air smelled like sagebrush and cedar, the way the sun made the back of my neck warm despite the chill.

"I reopened Haven and Harmony," I murmured.

Lemon's brows shot up. "Seriously?"

"Just a few small gigs. I've been picking up used furniture, refinishing it. Doing little redesigns around town. Olivia's been helping. Even built me some shelves last week."

"That's amazing."

"It's... weird. Letting myself want something again."

"It's overdue."

We sat like that for a while, letting the world around us quiet down. Birds rustled in the brush. Distant cows groaned across the pasture. The sky shifted again, slanting into gold.

"I missed you," I said finally.

She didn't say it back. She just wrapped an arm around my shoulder and pulled me in; my head tucked awkwardly against her hoodie.

When the sun finally dipped below the hills and the wind got sharp enough to make us shiver, she tossed the blanket over our laps and said, "You're staying for dinner. I'm making enchiladas and you're not allowed to argue."

I let her lead me back to the cab. My chest still ached, but not the same way it used to. Not like it was caving in. More like it was stretching, relearning its shape.

Smoke and Mirrors

The door to the hardware store groaned as I pushed it open, the scent of mulch and fertilizer thick in the air. I blinked against the blast of cold from the industrial AC and made for the paint aisle, the list I'd scribbled onto the back of a grocery receipt folded between my fingers. Light switch covers. Cabinet pulls. Sample pots of cream-colored satin. Nothing fancy. Nothing showy. Just enough to make the latest client's tiny rental feel like a home.

The store was mostly quiet, just a couple of employees restocking shelves and a kid dragging his feet behind a woman with a cart full of drywall compound. I paused to compare two knobs—matte black or aged brass—and held them both up to the light.

My phone buzzed in my back pocket. I pulled it out, glanced at the message from Olivia about chicken feed, and was slipping it back when I caught a flash of movement out of the corner of my eye.

Gray hoodie. Navy ball cap. Wide shoulders. That gait. A lazy sort of lope I knew too well.

My body went rigid before my brain caught up. Not him. He wasn't here. Couldn't be. But—

It wasn't Austin.

It was Nate. One of his old drinking buddies. The one who used to slap me on the back too hard when he came over. The one who always laughed too loud at Austin's worst jokes, and once told me I "talked prettier than I ought to." I hadn't seen him since the barbecue two summers ago where Austin had downed three beers in under an hour and glared at me the whole ride home because I'd laughed too long at someone else's story.

Nate was ten feet away, flipping through a bin of clearance extension cords. I had no idea if he'd seen me yet. My lungs locked up like they were trying to protect themselves from air. My hands trembled so slightly I almost didn't notice, until the metal knob tapped against the other in my palm.

I didn't move.

I didn't run.

I stood there, surrounded by paint samples, aisle signage, and that cloying fake pine smell, and I fucking stayed still.

My pulse screamed under my skin. My thoughts spun—what if he saw me? What if he told Austin? What if he still talked to him, still knew where he was, what was he capable of? What if this was just one more way Austin reached out, sent a piece of himself back into my world?

I reached for the shelf with slow, careful fingers and returned both knobs. They made a soft clink against the metal peg.

Nate shifted, stretched his arms overhead, and turned to walk toward the next aisle. He didn't look at me.

He didn't look at me.

I released a breath I hadn't known I was holding and immediately hated myself for doing it like that. I hated the way my mind turned into static, the way the muscles in my thighs ached from being half-ready to sprint. I hated that one man—one connection to him—could yank me back to that version of myself, the one who apologized before she even spoke.

But I didn't leave my cart behind. I didn't ditch the list. I walked it all out—aisle by aisle, picking what I needed, crossing things off. My steps weren't fast, but they were mine. Steady, firm, deliberate.

At the register, I paid in cash, exchanged small talk with the clerk about the weather, and took my receipt with dry fingers.

My phone buzzed again on the way out. Olivia asking if I wanted to grab lunch on the way home.

I typed back: Already heading to the truck. Let's eat.

The door let out its mechanical sigh as I pushed it open. Warm air hit my face. A bird darted across the lot. Tires crunched on gravel somewhere nearby.

I spotted the truck right away. Olivia's old Ford, dusty from the ranch roads and filled with reusable tote bags and feed sacks in the back. I climbed into the driver's seat and pulled the door closed, then sat with my hands on the wheel for a full minute before I started it.

I let myself feel it. The way my stomach clenched like a fist. The way my back still tingled from being watched, even though I hadn't been. I let myself sit with all of it.

Then I took a breath, long and shaky, and turned the key. The truck rumbled to life beneath me, solid, loud, and real. I shifted into reverse and eased out of the parking space.

I didn't look over my shoulder. Not even once.

By the time I pulled back into the ranch, my shoulders were locked up so tight I could barely lift my arms. Gravel popped beneath the tires as I parked beside the barn, I sat there with the truck idling, hands clenched around the wheel like it might bolt if I let go. My stomach had settled into a strange rhythm somewhere between buzzing and aching—too much adrenaline with nowhere to go. I cut the engine, pressed my forehead to the steering wheel for a breath, then forced myself out of the cab.

The late afternoon sun poured down hot and heavy across the fields, gold and dust mixing over the fencing rails. A few goats had gathered around a hay pile near the fence, chewing in lazy circles. The breeze tugged at my shirt, the hem fluttering where I'd half tucked it earlier. I felt like a scarecrow coming undone.

Olivia was out by the tack shed, crouched down near the hose spigot, boots planted wide and elbow-deep in a coil of something. I crossed the yard slower than I meant to, gravel biting at the soles of my shoes. I didn't say anything. Just stopped a few feet away and waited, arms crossed tight over my chest.

She looked up after another beat and squinted against the sun. "You okay?"

"Nope."

"Wanna tell me about it?"

"I saw someone from... back then. In town. One of his friends." My voice cracked halfway through—I hated it.

She stood, wiping her hands off on her jeans. "He say anything to you?"

"I don't think he saw me. But it was enough."

"Yeah," she said. Not dramatic. Just simple agreement, like she'd seen something like this before. She motioned toward the porch. "Come on. You look like you're about to shake yourself outta your skin."

I followed her up the steps, heart still thudding too fast, chest too tight. Inside, the kitchen was quiet except for the hum of the fridge and the soft creak of the old fan turning slow above the table. I dropped into the chair closest to the window and pressed my fingertips to my temples.

She poured two glasses of sweet tea without asking. The ice clinked as she set one in front of me.

"I didn't run," I said, after a while. "I thought about it. My body really wanted to. But I didn't."

"That's because you're brave," she said, pulling her chair back with a thump. "Doesn't always look like what they tell you it does. Sometimes, it's just standing there and not falling apart."

"I still feel like I fell apart."

"Maybe. But you stayed upright." She took a drink and leaned back, her boots up on the rung of the chair across from her. "You could've ducked out, disappeared, panicked. Instead, you did what you came to do, then drove yourself back here. That's more than most people manage."

The back of my throat burned. "I keep thinking it'll get easier. That I'll stop reacting like this."

"Maybe. But that doesn't mean the way you react now is wrong. Your body's still catching up to what your brain already knows. You're safe now."

I didn't know what to say to that. So, I drank the tea.

She let the silence stretch without trying to fill it. That was one of the things I appreciated about her—she didn't press, didn't try to fix things with platitudes. She just made space.

"Do you think I'm ever going to feel normal again?"

"I think you're gonna feel better than that," she said. "Normal's overrated. Half the time, it just means numb."

"I don't want to be numb anymore," I said. "I was numb for so long, I forgot what it was like to want anything."

She nodded like that made perfect sense. "Then we don't aim for numb. We aim for full."

I scoffed. "Full sounds terrifying."

"Yeah, well, most good things are." She finished her tea, then got up and grabbed the cookie tin from the top of the fridge. Set it on the table like it was the holy grail. "You earned one. Hell, maybe three."

"I'll take two and feel mildly guilty about it."

"Guilt doesn't count when the cookies are homemade."

I took one, bit into it, and let the sugar pull something gentle out of me. It was small, but it was something. I closed my eyes and let myself just sit, the noise in my head came down to a low hum. When I opened them, she was watching me the way she did sometimes—like she was checking for cracks in the foundation.

"You still thinking about going back to therapy this week?" she asked.

"Yeah. I think I need to."

"You're doing the work, you know. That's what matters."

"I know." I stared at the edge of the table. "But I still catch myself wondering if I should've stayed. If leaving really changed anything."

She leaned forward, palms flat. "Look at me."

I did.

"You're breathing different. Walking different. You smile sometimes without apologizing for it. You're decorating your damn room like it's your first dorm and you just discovered throw pillows. Don't tell me nothing's changed."

I let out a breath that might've been a laugh. "You noticed the pillows, huh?"

"They're fucking everywhere. It's like a pastel explosion. Not subtle."

"I like soft things now."

"You've always liked soft things. You just weren't allowed to have them."

That shut me up. I didn't argue, because she was right. I hadn't let myself admit it out loud, but I'd traded softness for survival. Now I was trying to find my way back to the things

I used to love without being afraid someone would rip them away.

We sat there until the shadows stretched long across the tile and the sun started to dip below the barn roof outside. Olivia stood and rinsed her glass.

"You coming out to help feed the horses?"

"Yeah, just give me a minute."

She nodded and left me to it.

I stayed at the table; fingers curled around the glass. My heart had slowed. My breath was steady. I wasn't looking out the window every two seconds. That felt like something.

Eventually, I pushed the chair back and stood, joints creaking. The fear was still there, coiled quiet and low, but it wasn't steering me anymore. I headed out the door, boots crunching on the path toward the barn, and the air smelled like sun-warmed hay and old wood.

Tomorrow might be worse. Or better. Or nothing at all. But today, I stayed. I stood my ground. I said, no to running.

THE HOLLOW GOODBYE

I STARTED THE LETTER on a Tuesday, sitting cross-legged on Olivia's porch with an old notepad balanced against my knee, and a pen I'd borrowed from the drawer near the coffee filters. The sun was low and thick across the pasture, the horses lazy in their movements, tails flicking in slow arcs. I sat with sweat collecting at the small of my back and didn't move for a long time. The pen stayed capped. My hand hovered, waiting for the first word to spill. But it didn't come easy.

It wasn't that I didn't know what to say. I knew exactly what I wanted to tell him. I'd just spent so long swallowing those words that letting them out felt unnatural, like learning how to breathe underwater. But eventually, I uncapped the pen, pressed it to the paper, and started writing.

I didn't think. I didn't stop to reread, or cross anything out. I just wrote, like the words had been sitting in my ribcage for years, and now they were clawing their way out.

You always liked to say I was dramatic.

You called me needy. Said I needed too much, wanted too much. That I made things bigger than they were. And I believed you. For too long, I believed maybe I was broken, and you were the only one who knew how to fix me. I shrank myself until I fit the version of me you wanted—quiet, agreeable, small.

I wrote through a dozen interruptions—Olivia walking past with a bucket of feed, the goats knocking something over in the barn, my phone buzzing on the table behind me—but I didn't stop. My hand cramped. My shoulders ached. The words didn't let up.

You said, I was lucky you put up with me. That nobody else ever would. You picked apart my laugh, my clothes, the way I said thank you to cashiers. You rolled your eyes when I ordered decaf, mocked me for needing naps, made me feel stupid for crying during commercials. None of it was ever direct, never loud enough to be obvious. Just enough to make me question myself. To make me think I was the problem.

You didn't raise your voice when you first pushed me. Just used that calm, slow tone like I'd done something to deserve it. Like you were disappointed. Like I should apologize for bruising. You always had a reason. I was late. I didn't answer my phone. I made you look stupid. And I started apologizing for everything—even things you never said out loud. I learned to anticipate your moods better than my own. I stopped calling my sister. I stopped taking jobs you didn't approve of. I stopped wearing yellow because you said it made me look washed out.

I pressed harder on the pen until the loops of my handwriting dug into the paper like scars.

But you don't get to do that anymore.

I left. You didn't think I would. You thought you'd broken me for good, didn't you? But I left anyway. I walked out and I didn't come back. And yes, I was scared—I still am. You made me live in fear long enough that it takes time to rewire my instincts. But I'm doing it. I'm unlearning you.

And here's the part you won't like—I'm doing okay. No, better than okay. I'm coming back to life. I'm laughing without waiting for permission. I'm decorating rooms again. I got a goddamn tattoo. I started saying no, and meaning it. I've got people in my life now who love me, without needing to control me. Who think I'm enough, exactly as I am.

You don't get to decide who I am anymore.

I stared at that last sentence for a long time. My hand hovered at the end of it, unsure whether to keep going or stop. There was more I could say. I could've listed every bruise, every door slam, every lie he told to twist me into someone obedient. I could've dissected the years he stole from me. But something about that last line felt final. Like a closing door.

I tore the page from the pad, folded it cleanly down the middle, and held it between my hands.

The air smelled like cut hay and early summer. A fly buzzed near my ankle. I blinked hard and sat with the letter a little longer before getting up and heading inside.

The house was quiet. Olivia was in the living room, booted feet propped on the ottoman, flipping through one of her ranch supply catalogs like it was a thriller novel. She looked up as I stepped in, and tilted her head.

"You look like you've just run a marathon," she said.

"Might've."

I walked over and held out the letter.

She didn't ask what it was. Just took it and read while I stood, arms crossed tight across my chest, heart thudding louder than it had when I saw that friend of his at the store.

Watching someone else read your pain isn't easy. It's a different kind of raw.

Olivia didn't make a sound. Her eyes moved steady over the page. No gasps. No muttered commentary. When she finished, she folded the letter again, slowly, precisely, then looked up at me.

"You want me to keep this?"

"No. I just... I wanted someone else to see it. To know it existed. Then, I think I'm gonna burn it."

She nodded. "You want company for that?"

"Yeah," I said. "Yeah, I do."

I knelt beside the fire pit and held the letter to the edge of the flame. It curled and blackened, the edges crisping faster than I imagined. Flames licked upward, fragile and deliberate, as if they'd been waiting for this. I didn't quiver. I held it steady.

Olivia sat next to me, gazing at the fire. Her shoulders relaxed into the denim jacket she'd probably dusted off just to sit here with me. Neither of us spoke.

The letter crackled, then sagged, then folded into pale ash. Tiny bits drifted off into the night breeze, caught midair by glowing embers. It didn't feel like an erasure. It wasn't a magic trick. It just felt like letting pieces go that were never mine to keep.

I fought the urge to swallow tears. My throat stung, but not in an old familiar way. This wasn't grief. This was release.

The fire slowed. Coals pressed red in their banks. The barn cast a soft shadow behind us, rough boards catching the last of dusk. Crickets began their evening song.

Olivia nudged my arm gently with hers. "That's okay."

I nodded and tucked my hands into my knees, letting the night air fill in the spaces trembling on the edges of my chest.

We sat there until the coals dimmed. Then she stood and led me inside. The lights were dim—but steady—like the rest of the house welcomed us back. I followed, blinking against the soft glow.

She grabbed two mugs and filled them with hot tea. I took mine with both hands, warmth seeping into my fingers replacing the burn of where the fire had been. I sat on the couch; she settled at the edge, close enough to look at.

"It's done, huh?"

I traced the rim. "Yeah. Done."

She adjusted the blanket across my lap. "You made it through the fire. Now you get to build around the ashes."

I drank the tea slowly. Bitter sweetness. I felt alive enough to taste it.

We didn't need noise. No music or chatter. Just breathing, mugs, and night. Somehow that quiet spoke louder than words I'd screamed on pages.

When I finally tipped my head back and closed my eyes, it wasn't sedation. It was assertion. I belonged. I belonged away from that life.

I stayed on the couch longer than usual. Didn't push the world away. I let my mind rest, unthreaded from survival.

"I'm proud of you," Olivia said softly, so warm I felt it in my eyelashes.

"Thank you," I whispered, voice soft as feathers.

She smiled, leaned her head on my shoulder.

We remained there until the house felt too quiet. The night sky pressed glass at the windows. I didn't move to get up. Fear didn't flare. It didn't pinch at my ribs.

There was only silence. And that was enough.

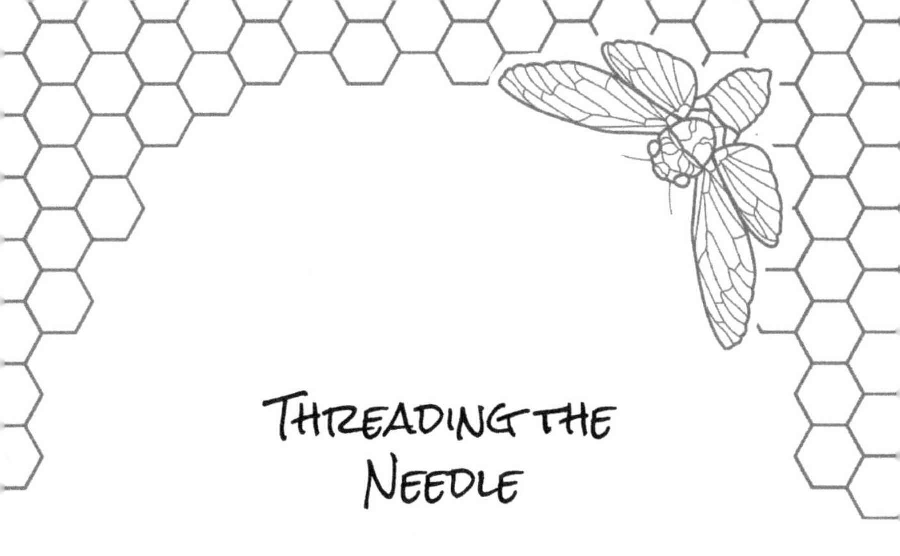

Threading the Needle

OLIVIA INVITED ME INTO the living room the morning after I burned the letter, handed me a steaming cup of coffee, and said, "I want you to redesign this house." I blinked—milk froth blurring my line of sight for a second—but when I refocused, she was sitting on the couch, sketchbook open across her knees like she meant it. Her smile wasn't teasing. It was hopeful.

The ranch house had always felt worn out—faded curtains, peeling paint on the rails yet sturdy enough for us to lean on. I stood in the middle of the living room and breathed it in: the slope of the ceiling beams, the sag in the carpet, the way the morning light cut across the floor in golden strips. I felt both terrified and electrified. This wasn't just another client's home. It belonged to her. It belonged to us.

She passed me a stack of index cards titled "Olivia's Life in Layers." I flipped through: Horses. Ranch hands who know your name. Sunrise coffee on the porch. Wind in the hay. Old books you can trust. Those were her offerings. Mine was, how I'd lost sight of home and found it again through color, and canvas, and reclaimed rooms.

We started with the front room. I pulled off a long roll of freezer paper, taped it to the floor and map-drew zones: vintage couch, rug, reading nook, horse portrait above the hearth. I laid swatches out: deep moss green, sand linen, ochre goldenrod. She sniffed each canvas remnant, crumpled the papers in delight or doubt, whispered things like, "that one feels like Rustlers Ridge at sundown."

We rambled through the day—measuring with sweat glistening on my forehead and her grabbing tools, like she ran things by instinct. We made lunch early out of a cooler: turkey wraps, damp hand towels, drifting cicada hum and sky. I sketch-scribbled between bites, idea on top of idea, drawing note arcs between table and chair and light path. My chest felt full—this was how I used to feel.

By dinner, we'd moved sofas just so. Lamps stood out like beacon posts. Curtains velcroed open to let the breeze stretch in, too. I placed a lemon throw pillow, winked at how yellow had become an act of resistance. Olivia dropped straw across the porch table and handed me a plate of chili, saying, "This is our by-hand-by-heart setup."

I set up night lights and walked through the house with her. We stood in the dining room, now washed in soothing blue, with shadow play from the chandelier. She touched my arm and said softly, "You made this mine too." I nodded, stomach knotting again, because it mattered in ways I'd almost forgotten.

The next day I busied myself: visits to a thrift store for reclaimed mirrors, negotiations with a woodworker for a custom sideboard on a ranch scale, texting the couple in Provo to ask if the brass fixtures they ordered still fit the vibe I'd drawn in my sketches. I worked between days: ironing linen curtains in her breezeway, center-placing a vintage rug that whispered nostalgia underfoot. I brushed horsehair off the sofa pillows, let them rest like old friends greeting me back.

I found myself humming lines I used to think prophetic—old country songs about returning, about resilience—while I arranged a display of horse prints and a macramé piece she made as a girl. I didn't worry if I messed up. I'd leveled beyond caring about perfection. I cared about homage, about honest intention.

Olivia asked me to design the bedroom too. I hesitated—low ceiling, weird angle. But when I placed the first fabric sample, and the first sketch board got pinned up, I felt it land. We added layered lights—old sconces from a rusted feed shop, which we repainted soft copper so they glowed, instead of shone. I taught her to shift bedding so the pillows were always inviting. She said, it felt like breathing again.

We worked through meals—she made fresh herbs and corn-bread, and I'd come behind with color boards; she'd say aloud what the hues made her ponder. She paused at one swatch, hand drifting, and sighed, "That yellow—your yellow. Sunshine." I didn't correct her, only tucked it in.

One afternoon, she asked for a "girls' day." We slipped into town, had iced tea under shade trees, then wandered a garden shop turning plants into gifts for rooms. We found tall snake plants and curling grasses for corners, and I wielded paint caps and indoor vases while she pulled pot after pot. Carrying armloads back, we laughed until our sides ached like we hadn't stopped for years.

Back at the ranch, I placed each plant where it belonged—one by the guest desk, one near the window seat; the greens softened edges of walls that had always felt harsh. She watched me breathe slow, nodding like each move healed a different part.

Night came on the porch with strings of lights I'd hung earlier. That glow pooled off the walls and the newly painted door. I stirred lemonade, slid in mint, and watched as the rooms finally began to reflect stories—our combined stories, not just functional space.

We sat on the lawn with blankets and took in the house—the front-gable windows lit, warm gold from inside. I pressed a hand against my heart, skin wide and tingling. Then, just inside, I saw a painting I'd made—abstract of cicada wings and pasture dust—leaned against the entry. I smiled.

She passed the cold mug and said, "You built more than decor. You built feeling."

I wanted to say I was still afraid—fear never fully released its grip—but I held back. Instead, I whispered, "I feel like me out here."

Cicada ink pressed with pride across arm, cortex pulsing like verification. The raw edges—fires, letters, scars—wove through these walls as texture now, not hurt. Each sample seized, each sketch refined, each paint swatch chosen—not for safety but because it felt right.

We didn't clean up fully that night. We just sat, in a silence that felt full. The earth cooled, the wind rustled the branches. Her dog lay low across the steps. I leaned into her shoulder. She didn't push me away. She didn't hush my past. She folded it in—layered it like boards, stained bronze and beautiful. And I didn't shrink. I filled the space I carved. I first thought it was courage. Olivia corrected: "Courage isn't crashing through things. Sometimes it's just reclaiming them."

I looked at the porch lights flickering. The farmhouse windows glowing. The rust of the cabinetry, the pull of the pillows. I felt shape again. I felt trust again. I felt color may come back—maybe wild enough to get loud—but not loud unless I allowed it.

That night, as I collapsed into the guest room—heavy legs, cheer cracking but not crumbling—I saw the cicada painting leaning by the door. I felt its wings stretch. And I stretched, too—muscle memory aligning with heart memory. My design spells weren't about pretty finishes. They were statements: I stayed. I built. I became.

Redrafted, restored, real.

And I still had rooms to fill.

We were down to the little things now—hooks for hats, trays for keys, art for the narrow hallway which always felt like a tunnel. Olivia brought out a stack of wrapped canvases she'd found at a yard sale the week before, each one a little chipped around the edges, but full of character. She had the kind of eye that saw potential in what most people walked past. I unwrapped one with a watercolor horse—streaks of gray and rust that made it look more myth than animal—and leaned it against the wall. My fingertips tingled just looking at it, like the color itself stirred something up.

She brought in a step stool and passed me the hammer. "You're taller," she said, grinning.

"I'm also clumsy," I shot back, but took it anyway. My shoulders ached from painting earlier in the day, but it felt good—earned. I balanced on the second step and held the frame steady while she stood below with a level, calling out when it was crooked. We argued, teased, bickered. But we laughed, too—really laughed. I hadn't heard myself do that without flinching in years.

We made a rhythm out of it. Hang, step back, tilt, rehang, argue, laugh. Then do it again. The hallway went from bare to lived-in in less than an hour. She stepped away to grab drinks while I stayed back to stare at what we'd done. The late-night shadows stretched along the floorboards, soft and long, and I watched the light shift across one of the old brass sconces we'd salvaged from a thrift store. The imperfections in the glass threw flecks across the wall, like confetti caught midair.

When she returned, she held out a piece of yellow sidewalk chalk and said, "Before we call it, I want you to do something."

I blinked. "What?"

"Sign the beam." She motioned to the one that ran across the hallway ceiling, just high enough that we'd both have to stretch. "Right there. It's your work. I want it marked."

My throat got tight. I looked up at the beam. There were old nail holes, faint scuff marks, the kind of wood grain that ran like stories across its length. "Won't that look stupid?"

She raised an eyebrow. "You asking me for design advice now?"

I rolled my eyes, but my chest burned warm. I climbed the stool again and hesitated, the chalk dusty in my grip.

"You don't have to write your name," she added. "Write whatever matters."

So, I did. I wrote one word—one I hadn't claimed for a long time. Free.

When I stepped down and looked at it, I didn't want to cry. I didn't want to crumble. I just stared at the soft yellow streaks and felt still. Like my hands weren't shaking anymore. Like I didn't have to apologize for anything.

We didn't say much after that. Just drifted into the living room with two glasses of sweet tea and sat on the floor. The couch cushions were still off to the side, mid-rearrangement. The room smelled like lemon cleaner, upholstery fabric, and late summer.

She flicked on the record player, and an old Emmylou Harris album started playing, the kind of song that stretched long, slow, and honest. I leaned back against the coffee table and watched the ceiling fan turn. She nudged me with her foot and asked, "You good?"

I thought about lying. I thought about softening it. But I didn't. "Getting there," I said instead.

Her head tilted. "Closer than you were?"

"Yeah. A hell of a lot closer."

We sat there until the record ran out. Just the two of us in a room that used to feel like someone else's but now carried our fingerprints all over it—every throw pillow, every nicked-up side table, every screw we'd tightened together. I remembered what my therapist said a few weeks ago—that healing wasn't always loud, or obvious. Sometimes it looked like doing dishes without crying. Sometimes it looked like signing a beam with yellow chalk.

The next morning, sunlight spilled over the wood floors, lighting the space like a stage. I stood in the hallway again, coffee in hand, staring at the art, the rug, the sconces, and the tiny yellow word tucked into the beam like a whisper. I felt something shift—not completely, not like I was fixed. But like I was standing on solid ground again.

Later, we hauled more boxes from the barn. Olivia insisted on keeping me busy, and I didn't argue. Movement helped. We found an old tin trunk filled with junk—trophies, broken light switches, a photo of her and her brother I hadn't seen before. She passed me the picture, then looked away quickly. I didn't ask. I just kept sorting.

We set up a new nook near the front door: a bench and hooks for coats, a small lamp beside it with a basket of dried lavender. It didn't match perfectly, but it felt right. I caught her smiling at it later.

By mid-afternoon, we took a break under the cottonwood out back. I pulled my hair up, leaned against the porch post, sweat clinging beneath my collar. She tossed me a cold bottle of water and flopped into a chair with a groan.

"My back's gonna be yelling at me for days," she muttered.

I snorted. "Yours? I'm the one who lugged that bookshelf up the stairs."

"You insisted," she shot back.

"Because you put the heavy end on me."

She grinned around her sip of water, and I couldn't stop smiling. My cheeks hurt from it, but I didn't care. I was sore, filthy, exhausted—and I felt more like myself than I had in years.

By evening, we had just one room left: the hallway leading to the guest room. I wanted to hang something personal there. Not generic, not thrifted. Something real.

I dug out an old sketchbook I hadn't touched in forever. Flipped past half-finished designs, water-stained pages, shaky lines. Then I found one I'd drawn last winter, when I thought I'd never leave. A sketch of a window cracked open, with light spilling in and curtains moving like breath. I didn't know why I'd drawn it back then. I knew now.

I framed it.

When we hung it up, Olivia looked at it for a long time, then said, "That's your way out, huh?"

"Yeah," I said. "Guess so."

The rest of the night was quiet. We cleaned up tools, folded extra blankets, turned off room lights, one by one. When I passed back through the hallway, I touched the beam again—my chalk word still there, faint but unmoved.

Before bed, I stood in the guest room doorway. My bags were still there; half unpacked like I was waiting for some invisible shoe to drop. I reached down and zipped the last one closed. Not because I was leaving. But because I didn't have to live ready to run anymore.

When I climbed into bed, my muscles groaned. My hands were covered in little scrapes and smudges. My fingernails were chipped. My back ached. But my chest didn't.

I stared at the ceiling and let the silence settle without bracing for it to snap. No footsteps upstairs. No vibrating phone. Just the hum of night, the rustle of wind, the slow unfurling of my own life, finally being mine again.

Roots Run Deep

THE TRUCK DOOR GROANED as I pushed it open, metal protesting like it hadn't been moved in years. I parked just off the gravel shoulder outside the old gate, where the dirt turned familiar, where the fence bowed slightly like it remembered who used to climb over it. Rustlers Ridge looked smaller than I remembered, but then again, maybe I was bigger now. Not taller. Just different. More of myself than I used to be.

I didn't bring anything with me. No bag, no notebook, no plan. Just me, the keys in my pocket, and the long stretch of land ahead that still somehow smelled like childhood and wildfire and summer rain. I rested my hand on the top rail of the fence and looked out over the pasture. Dry patches, low grass, a handful of grazing horses off in the distance. One of them lifted its head and stared like it knew me.

I walked the fence line slowly, letting my boots kick up dust. Each step felt careful, but not hesitant. Just deliberate. I knew where I was, even if my body remembered it more clearly than my brain did. The rocks still stuck out at weird angles by the second post near the bend. The old oak tree still split the light strangely where the branches tangled overhead. I paused when I reached the slope that led toward the barn and breathed in deep. Sage. Dry earth. Faint traces of hay. My eyes stung, but I didn't cry.

The wind picked up just enough to push my hair into my face, and I tucked it behind my ear as I kept walking. There was a rhythm to it—boots on packed dirt, gate chains rattling faintly behind me, the flap of some metal sheet on the barn's roof. I thought of all the years I'd spent pretending I'd never come back here. How long I avoided anything that made me remember. And now here I was, following the same path I used to take when I needed to be alone. Only this time, I didn't feel lost.

The barn came into view, slumped a little more than it used to be, the siding a little more silvered with age. One shutter hung crooked above the loft, and someone had painted over the rust on the latch with a dull black coat that now flaked at the edges. I ran my fingers across the door as I opened it. It still stuck halfway. Still scraped the floor like it always had. The sound echoed across the hollow space inside.

Dust swirled in lazy spirals across the floorboards, and my boots kicked it up as I stepped inside. The temperature dropped instantly—cooler under the shade, quieter too. I let my eyes adjust as I walked toward the tack room, the back of my throat tight and dry. The horses weren't here anymore. Most of the stalls were empty, but the scent of them lingered—leather, straw, old grain. Like the ghost of a memory that hadn't been given permission to leave yet.

The door to the tack room was half open. I pushed it gently, slow enough that the hinges didn't squeal. Inside, everything looked smaller. The shelves were still lined with bits and brushes, though a lot of the gear had been moved, or cleared out. The leather straps hung limp from their hooks. A few old saddle blankets were folded in the corner, faded with dust. I turned toward the back wall and crouched low, brushing my hand across the old wooden panel until I found it—barely visible now, half-covered with grime and weather. Our initials, carved when we were maybe ten or eleven. L & H. Lemon had drawn a wonky heart around them. It looked more like a potato now. But it was still there.

My fingers traced it slowly, and my heart thudded against my ribs like it was trying to keep pace with something it had forgotten how to measure. I didn't cry. I didn't smile. I just breathed, steady and quiet, and let myself feel what came. It wasn't sadness. Not exactly. It was something quieter. Something that sat next to me like a tired friend, not asking for anything. Just being there.

I sank down onto the floor, legs folding beneath me, and leaned back against the rough boards. Light streamed through a crack above the door, hitting a hook on the far wall and throwing a streak of brightness across the dust in the air. I watched it shift while my body slowly unclenched, like I'd been holding something in without knowing it and it was finally loosening its grip.

I remembered climbing up into the loft to read alone. I remembered throwing hay down with Lemon, getting straw in my bra and cussing about it for hours after. I remembered a time I stormed out here after a fight with my mom and sat on the fence until the sun dipped low and I couldn't see my own hands. Those memories didn't hurt the way they used to. They didn't pull me under. They just existed, part of the fabric now, like old stitching in a well-loved quilt.

The sound of a creaking board somewhere in the barn startled me slightly, but I didn't jolt or flinch. I just listened. Probably the wind. Probably time reminding me to get up, move forward, keep going.

I stood slowly, knees popping like firewood. I dusted off my jeans and smoothed my shirt, then ran my hand over our initials one last time before I turned and stepped back into the barn.

The light outside had changed—warmer, lower. I walked out into the yard and turned to look at the barn again. It wasn't just a relic. It wasn't just a chapter. It was a place I'd lived. A place I'd left. A place I could return to without losing myself.

I walked back toward the fence, the sun dragging long, golden shadows across the dirt like ribbons. The field hummed with crickets and the low rustle of wind cutting through the dry grass. The air smelled like baked sage and cracked earth, and for a minute, I just let it fill my lungs. Not because I needed grounding or a tool from therapy or anything else practical. Just because I wanted to. Because it felt good.

The fence rail was weathered smooth where generations of kids—me included—had climbed and perched, dared each other to jump or yell at the sky. I slid one boot onto the bottom rung, hoisted myself up without much grace, and swung a leg over to sit at the top. My thighs pressed against the hot wood, and I leaned forward just slightly, arms resting on my knees. The air was still warm, even as the sun lowered, but it had that early fall coolness around the edges. That barely-there warning that summer was almost over. I watched a horse out in the far pasture flick its tail, head buried in the grass, disinterested in the rest of the world.

It was quiet in the kind of way I hadn't let myself experience in years. Not the hush of fear or hiding. Just quiet. The kind where you could hear your own heartbeat and it didn't race. I looked out across the land and didn't flinch. Didn't search for a shadow behind every tree. Didn't wonder who was following or what was going to be taken next. The panic that used to live just under my skin had quieted into something else entirely—something steadier. Still wary, but not gasping anymore.

This field, this barn, that crooked fence post down by the creek, they'd all been here before I knew what survival meant. Before I knew how sharp silence could feel in the wrong house. Before I understood what it was to question every version of myself someone else handed me. The dirt under my boots didn't ask for anything. It didn't expect me to apologize for coming back different.

I traced my finger along the splintered wood beside me. Thought about how much time I'd spent here as a teenager pretending, I'd end up anywhere else but Utah. How I used to dream myself out of this place, convinced it was too small, too dusty, too full of everything I wanted to forget. But now, it felt like the opposite. Like it had been waiting for me to get my shit together and remember who I was. Not someone's girlfriend. Not someone's punching bag, or trophy, or project. Just me.

My legs swung a little, heels tapping the fence in a lazy rhythm. I let my shoulders drop and my chest expand. I didn't need to force anything. The land wasn't going anywhere. Neither was I. Not yet, anyway.

A breeze swept through and lifted my hair off the back of my neck. I closed my eyes and tilted my face up toward the fading light, let it warm my cheeks. There were still things to figure out—where I'd live long-term, how I'd keep the design business running without folding under pressure again, what came next when the adrenaline wasn't driving me anymore. But none of it felt impossible. Maybe messy. Maybe unpredictable. But not impossible.

I stayed on the rail a while longer, listening to the wind and the faint creak of the barn shifting behind me. Somewhere far off, a bird called out. A low whistle, sharp and deliberate. Then silence again. The kind that didn't feel like loneliness anymore. Just space.

Eventually, I climbed down, boots landing solid in the dirt. My legs didn't wobble. I didn't hesitate or look back at the barn like it owed me something. I just walked forward. Toward the truck. Toward the gravel road. Toward whatever came next.

I slid into the driver's seat and sat there for a second with the engine off. The key rested in my hand. The metal was cool against my palm, grounding. I looked out the windshield at the open stretch of road ahead. It didn't intimidate me like it used to. I wasn't looking for escape anymore.

I turned the key, the engine rumbling to life beneath me. Dust kicked up as the tires rolled forward, the ranch growing smaller in the rearview mirror. I didn't need to bring the past with me. It had already done its work.

I drove steady, hands sure on the wheel, the sky deepening into shades of rust and violet. The last sliver of sunlight dipped low behind the hills, and I didn't chase it. I just followed the road, windows cracked, the scent of sage still clinging to my clothes.

I wasn't returning to who I used to be.

I was heading toward who I finally was.

The Weight of Wings

THE FIRST TIME I stepped into the building, the dust clung to the light like it was holding its breath. Plaster curled off the corners of the walls, and the floor creaked with every step. It smelled like neglect—wood rot, old paint, stale air—but something about it tugged at me. Not in a romantic way, not like some cheesy transformation show where everything was just a coat of paint away from being fixed. It was real work. It was ruin and potential mixed together. That's what made it feel worth doing.

The women who ran the nonprofit met me there just before noon, all of them balancing clipboards and iced coffees. They were kind, busy, a little frazzled, and clearly out of their depth when it came to construction or design. One of them handed me a key. Just like that, it was mine to shape.

I walked the perimeter alone, brushing my fingertips across the brick near the entrance, scuffing my boots over the splinters of old vinyl flooring. It had once been a dentist's office—ugly, fluorescent, clinical. But there was light pouring in from the south-facing windows, and that was enough to work with. I closed my eyes and let myself see it how it could be.

Not a sterile place full of check-in counters and cold chairs. A place for softness and safety and breath. For women like me—women who had survived things they hadn't even known how to name at the time. Women who needed more than pity and pamphlets. A place that wouldn't fix them, just hold them.

I spent the next few days obsessing over layout sketches at Olivia's kitchen table, pencil tucked behind my ear, sleeves pushed up to my elbows, forgetting to eat until my stomach protested loud enough to make her come nudge me with a sandwich. I rearranged every line a dozen times. Open shelving for visibility. Natural wood tones for grounding. Textured fabric in warm ochre, rust, and yellow. Nothing sharp. No overhead lights unless they were diffused. I wanted it to feel like an exhale. Like quiet bravery. Like you could walk in and finally unclench your jaw.

The work was slow. I didn't have a crew—just a few hired hands and whoever I could talk into helping me carry in tile, or hang shelves. Olivia showed up most weekends, always with snacks and loud opinions about throw pillow patterns. Once, she brought her ranch foreman along, and he installed three light fixtures without saying more than ten words. We played music off a busted Bluetooth speaker and argued about which playlist was better. The days blurred together with sawdust and coffee and splatters of paint I stopped trying to wipe off my arms.

One afternoon, I stood in the middle of what would be the main lounge space, paint roller in hand, music off. The air was thick with the scent of drying primer. The windows were open, the breeze pushing at the drop cloths like restless ghosts. My thighs ached from crouching and standing, my neck from looking up too long. But I was exactly where I wanted to be. I looked around and saw it—the version that had only existed in my head weeks ago, now halfway real.

The walls were done in a soft beige, warm without being boring. One wall was dedicated to open shelving—books, ceramic mugs, plants with wide leaves—and above it, a mural was taking shape, still faint in pencil outlines. I'd asked a local artist to help me with it: vines, abstract figures, something that felt like community without needing to spell it out. I ran my hand across the dried paint beside the entry and smiled without thinking.

The next day, I laid rugs. They came rolled tight, stiff with newness, but once unwrapped they settled, like they belonged.

I flopped down on one of them, let my spine meet the floor. The ceiling above had wooden beams that I'd almost painted white, but left raw at the last minute. It was better that way. Honest. Textured. Worn.

I thought about how every inch of this space felt like a map. Yellow accents like the cardigan I'd bought months ago, like the journal that sat on my nightstand. Earth tones to mirror the ridges near the ranch. Rounded corners because I didn't want anyone brushing against something sharp without warning. It was mine, even if my name wasn't on the building.

The couches were delivered the day after the muralist started painting. They were heavy, but a few volunteers helped muscle them into place. One woman, a therapist who would be renting one of the back offices, brought me lemonade in a mason jar and said, "This feels like a place I'd want to cry in." It was the best compliment I'd ever gotten.

As we worked, she told me about her clients, her passion for helping women who didn't see their own strength. She didn't press me for my story. Just shared hers like an offering and left space between her sentences. It was rare, that kind of quiet generosity.

When the front desk went in, I refused to let it become a barrier. No glass. No sliding window. Just a wooden surface with a vase of fresh flowers and a handwritten welcome sign. I taped it up myself, hands shaking a little, but not from nerves.

Just energy. The kind that used to eat me alive, now channeled into something that would outlast me.

The final piece was a series of framed quotes. Not the cheesy kind you find in bargain bins, but ones I'd gathered over time. One of them was mine, written on a post-it during a particularly hard night: "You're allowed to be soft and still survive." I printed it in block letters and tucked it between a photo of wild horses and a pressed flower. Hung the frame by the bathroom door where people would see it on their way in and out.

The day I finished, it was just me and the quiet. No music, no laughter, just the hum of the HVAC and the click of my boot heels on the floor as I walked through every room. I touched everything. The desk. The shelf. The edge of a blanket folded neatly on the back of the couch. Every choice had been deliberate. Every corner told a different version of the same story: I lived. I escaped. I built something that made space for other people to do the same.

I ran my hands along the armrest of one chair, then sat, legs curled under me. Outside, the street was busy—horns, footsteps, the low thrum of tires over asphalt—but inside, it was still. Not sterile. Not tense. Just still. My chest rose and fell without catching. My palms stayed dry.

This place didn't need to scream. It just had to hold people.

I leaned my head back and looked at the ceiling beams. Not perfect, not even, but solid. Real.

I stayed there a long while before reaching for the final piece: a small, ceramic bowl I'd made in a pottery class years ago, long before things got complicated. I set it on the table by the entrance, filled it with yellow glass stones I'd found at a thrift shop. They caught the light just enough to glow.

Then I stepped back, hands on my hips, heart thudding slow and sure. My muscles ached from the work, my shirt was stained, and my hair was half tied up in a sad knot—but I didn't care. I wasn't performing. I was just here.

I turned off the lights, locked the door behind me, and walked out into the fading sun. My reflection caught briefly in the glass: tired, paint-streaked, smiling.

The space was ready. So was I.

The scissors were too big. Someone had borrowed them from a school theater department or a church or something, all ceremonial shine and dulled edges that probably wouldn't cut paper. The ribbon—yellow, because of course it was—hung taut between two hand-painted stands at the entrance, fluttering a little in the breeze. I'd double-checked the alignment that morning, kneeling in the parking lot with a level and painter's tape, re-tying the ends so they hung neat. Olivia told me to stop fussing and let it look lived in. I told her to hush and hold the other end still.

By late afternoon, a small crowd had gathered—friends, a few donors, volunteers from the local shelter, and some of the women who'd be using the space. Someone passed out lemonade in plastic cups. A kid tugged at the ribbon, then darted away laughing when one of the board members gently scolded him. I leaned against the wall near the door and tried not to look like I was bracing myself for impact.

A woman from the nonprofit stepped up and tapped the mic clipped to the folding podium. "We're here today to celebrate the opening of something really special," she started, then went into a short speech about the purpose of the space, the community, the vision for the future. I only heard maybe half of it. My heart was doing its own thing—slow at first, then suddenly too fast, like it was catching up to the moment and didn't know what to do once it got there.

When she waved me forward, I didn't move at first. Olivia nudged me hard in the ribs and handed me the big scissors. I stepped up, nodded at the crowd, and said, "Thanks for coming." It wasn't elegant, but it landed.

They clapped, cheered a little. I held the scissors like I had any business wielding them and cut the ribbon in two. The crowd applauded again, and just like that, the place was real. Official. Open.

Inside, the space buzzed with voices and footsteps, people trailing fingers along shelves, admiring the mural, picking up the throw pillows like they were treasures. I floated through conversations, smiling and answering questions, accepting compliments with the awkward half-nods of someone who wasn't used to being seen so clearly. I caught Olivia laughing in the kitchen nook with one of the artists and let the warmth of that settle in my chest.

One of the founders found me near the bookshelf and pulled me into a tight hug. "You made this a sanctuary," she said into my ear. Her voice cracked on the word. "It's what we dreamed of."

I held on a second longer before stepping back. "It already was. I just… translated it."

She smiled and blinked hard, then walked off to greet someone else. I stood there, hands in my pockets, watching as a woman sank onto one of the couches and immediately took off her shoes like she'd found home.

Later, after the crowd thinned, the lemonade was mostly gone, and someone started playing soft music over the little speaker we'd hidden behind a plant, I found a quiet spot in the back office and let myself breathe. The door was open, but no one came in. I sat in the desk chair, spun it slowly from side to side, and looked around at the room I'd furnished last, still getting used to its shape.

It was simple—just a desk, a small round table with mismatched chairs, a reading lamp, and a framed print of wildflowers. But every part of it had been chosen. Nothing borrowed. Nothing forced. I ran my hand along the edge of the table and thought about the woman that would use this space. What she'd bring into it. What she'd leave behind.

Olivia stuck her head around the doorway. "You hiding?"

"Maybe."

She came in and flopped onto the little couch across from me. "It's beautiful."

"Thanks."

"No, like, really. It's the kind of place you walk into and don't want to leave."

I looked down at my hands. Paint still clung to the skin around my fingernails, faint and stubborn. "I wasn't sure I could do it."

"Well, you did." She kicked her boots off and tucked one leg under the other. "And I know I've said this already, but I'm proud of you."

The words hit harder than I expected. I didn't answer right away. Just nodded and looked toward the window, where the last light was fading across the blinds in long, broken stripes.

She didn't push. Just sat with me, like always.

Eventually I said, "There were days I thought I was never gonna get back to this. Not just the work. I mean... giving a shit about anything. About people, color, lines, movement. All of it."

"You didn't just get back to it," she said. "You turned it into something new."

I turned that over. Let it settle.

"Think they'll keep the couch pillows arranged the way I showed them?" I asked, half grinning.

She barked a laugh. "Not a chance."

"Yeah. Probably not."

We both laughed, tired and easy. I could still hear a few guests lingering out front. One of them laughed, and it echoed faintly off the painted walls. There were crumbs on the rug from the cookies someone brought. The hallway light buzzed a little from overuse. The mural was finished.

It was perfect.

Eventually Olivia stood, stretched, and said, "Ready to head out?"

"Give me five."

She nodded and slipped out without another word. I stayed seated, listening to the soft thud of the door closing behind her. Then I stood, walked out into the main room, and ran my hand across the frame of the quote I'd hung by the bathroom.

"You're allowed to be soft and still survive."

I whispered it under my breath without meaning to, then laughed to myself. God, it was corny. But it was mine. I turned off the lights, one by one, leaving only the hallway lamp on behind me. The yellow bowl of glass stones on the entry table glowed faintly as I passed it.

Outside, the sky had gone dark, but the streetlights were bright, casting gold over the sidewalk. I stepped down the front steps and pulled the door shut behind me. Locked it. Held the key in my hand a little longer than I needed to.

Then I walked to the truck and drove off. Not home, not yet. But somewhere steady. Somewhere real.

The Honey Inside

THE BATHROOM SMELLED LIKE cedar and lavender. Not fancy—just the way the hand soap and shampoo happened to mix after a hot shower. The mirror above the sink was still streaked with little dots of steam, but enough had cleared that I could see myself plainly. I leaned forward, elbows on the counter, studying every detail like I hadn't been doing this same thing for weeks now. Months, maybe. Skin still healing in places, hair grown out past my shoulders again, no makeup to soften the edges.

Just me. No pretense, no performance. Tired eyes—but steadier than they used to be. Jaw relaxed. Shoulders down instead of hunched like they were bracing for something. I pulled the towel tighter around my body, then let it drop and reached for the sweatshirt I'd tossed onto the counter earlier. Yellow, like so many things lately—bright, soft, and worn at the cuffs. I slipped it over my head and let the fabric settle against my skin.

The morning had been quiet. I'd woken early and made tea instead of coffee, let Olivia sleep in for once. The kettle had clicked off and I'd stood there barefoot on the cold kitchen tile, cradling the mug like it was the only thing anchoring me to the room. No chaos, no noise. Just steam rising in front of the window and the faint sound of horses shifting in the pasture.

Now, in this small space where the light slanted through the high window just right, I ran my fingers over the small scar on my forearm—the one I used to cover with bracelets or sleeves, like it would vanish if I just ignored it long enough. I didn't cover it anymore. Didn't decorate it either. It was just part of the story now.

I tied my hair back messily, not caring if it was symmetrical or smooth. A few strands stuck out above my ears, I left them. No makeup today. No real plans. Just me and the barn chores, maybe a late lunch on the porch. I stared at myself again and whispered the name that used to belong to the little girl who climbed trees and whispered secrets to horses.

"Honey."

It came out shaky at first. Almost too soft to hear. My throat tightened. I tried again, firmer this time.

"Honey."

That time, it landed. Not as a ghost. Not as a wish. Just a truth. One that had always been there, even when I'd forgotten how to call it by name.

I watched myself say it a third time, lips moving like I was practicing for a reunion with someone I hadn't seen in years. My reflection didn't look startled anymore. Didn't look like she was waiting for permission. She just nodded, faintly, like she already knew.

I turned off the light and stepped into the hallway barefoot, the floor cool beneath me. The sweatshirt hung just past my hips; sleeves bunched at the wrists. My fingers grazed the yellow chalk mark I'd left on the beam last week, and for a second, I paused there, listening. Somewhere down the hall, Olivia's dog barked once, sharp and cheerful, probably chasing shadows. A few birds sang near the window above the stairs.

I kept walking. There wasn't anything dramatic about it—no triumphant music or tearful epiphany. Just the soft sound of my feet against the wood, the steady rhythm of my breath, and the solid, grounding truth of knowing who I was again.

Not broken. Not unfinished. Just... here. Alive. Awake. And mine.

The air outside was crisp enough to sting, but not enough to chase me back in. I stepped off the porch barefoot, wincing slightly as the cool dirt and gravel bit into my heels. The sweatshirt hung loose on me, sleeves half-covering my fingers, and I tucked my hands into the front pocket, pulling it snug against my ribs. I walked toward the field, letting the golden light stretch out ahead of me, long and warm across the grass.

The sky was one of those Utah skies that felt too big for the world, streaked with amber and soft blues, the sun peeking over the edge like it was just now remembering it had work to do. I stopped near the fence line and took a slow breath, the kind that settled somewhere deep in my chest. No pressure behind it. No panic crouched in my lungs. Just air. Cool and clean.

From the barn, Olivia's voice called out, something half-laughing, half-sarcastic about the hay bales being stacked crooked again. I shouted back that it wasn't me and she muttered something I couldn't hear, which probably meant she believed me. Or didn't care. Either way, she didn't call again. The hum of the ranch started up—boots scuffing on wood, the clink of tack, horses shifting restlessly in their stalls.

My phone buzzed in the front pocket of the sweatshirt. I pulled it out; thumb already smudged across the screen. A text from Lemon.

"One of the chickens stole my scrunchie. This is the hill I die on."

I snorted, typing back:

"She probably looks better in it than you."

A beat passed.

"Rude, but fair. I'll allow it."

I tucked the phone away, smiling into the collar of my sweat-shirt. The kind of smile that didn't feel forced. It cracked across my face slow and uneven, like it was rediscovering how to live there.

I leaned against one of the old posts, the wood still solid under my shoulder. From here I could see the spread of the field, horses grazing lazily in the far distance. One of the strays—the orange tabby that had adopted us two weeks ago—slipped between the fence slats and wound around my ankle. I bent down, scratched behind her ears, and she purred like she'd been waiting for me to remember she existed.

She darted off just as quickly, chasing something invisible.

The sweatshirt sleeves bunched around my elbows, and I shoved them back up again. My arms still carried faint outlines of old bruises, faded now into yellowed smudges. Most of them had already disappeared. Some might never go. But I didn't look away when I saw them anymore. Didn't tug my sleeves down to cover them like I was ashamed of what they'd meant.

I turned back toward the barn and started walking.

Inside, Olivia was leaning against a stall door, arms crossed over her chest, chewing on a granola bar like it had personally offended her.

"I stacked those straight," I said.

She raised a brow. "Yeah? Maybe in your imagination."

"I was distracted. The goat tried to eat my hair again."

"That goat has taste."

I rolled my eyes and ducked past her to grab a bucket. "Need me to muck stalls or refill water?"

"Pick your poison," she said, biting off the last chunk of the bar and tossing the wrapper into the trash by the door.

I opted for water and took the long way around the paddock. My boots sank slightly into the earth, softened by last night's rain. The scent of damp hay and manure and sunshine hit me all at once, familiar and grounding. The troughs weren't too bad, just low enough that the horses were getting impatient. One snorted near my ear as I tipped the hose into the first one.

I moved from stall to stall, elbow deep in farm chores, letting my thoughts wander where they wanted. I hadn't done that in a long time. Let them go unsupervised without worrying they'd turn on me.

They didn't.

They slid instead to the small things—the taste of tea earlier, the weight of the sweatshirt, the way Lemon's stupid chicken probably strutted around like it owned the damn place with that scrunchie on its head.

I thought about the nonprofit center in Provo, the one I'd finished decorating last week. It still didn't feel real—that I had done that. Not just the work itself, but the whole process: meeting with the women who ran the place, listening to what they needed, shaping something safe and soft and strong around them.

They'd hugged me when I left. Said I'd made something sacred out of brick and drywall.

It wasn't magic, what I'd done. Just choices. Intentional ones. Earth tones, plants that were hard to kill, lighting that didn't buzz or hum or flicker. Curtains instead of blinds. A reading nook. Yellow pillows. Yellow everywhere. I hadn't even noticed how much of it I'd used until I was fluffing one of the last cushions and realized it matched the cardigan I wore on my first visit.

I was halfway through rinsing out the second trough when Olivia stepped into the paddock.

"You're up early for someone who wasn't on the list."

"I'm never on the list. You just like bossing me around."

She grinned, squinting against the sun. "Yeah, well. You're easy to boss."

I flicked water at her and she yelped, backing away like it'd been acid.

"I swear to God, if you soak me—"

"Then what?"

"I'll lock you in the tack room again."

"That was one time and you lost the key."

"Still funny."

I shook my head and bent back over the hose, the grin refusing to leave my face.

When the chores were done, we wandered back toward the house together, boots muddy and shoulders relaxed. The dog—some mutt we hadn't named yet—trotted behind us, tail up like he was in charge.

"I was thinking about redoing the spare room," Olivia said as we climbed the porch steps. "Not that you have to stay forever. Just. I don't know. Feels like it could use a better paint job. And maybe some bookshelves."

I didn't answer right away. The door creaked open and we stepped inside, warm air and coffee smell wrapping around us like a worn blanket.

She didn't push.

Finally, I said, "You don't have to redo it on my account."

"I want to. You made this place beautiful. Least I can do is make one room feel like it belongs to you too."

I rubbed at the back of my neck, fingers catching on the little baby hairs there.

"I might go back to Rustlers Ridge again next week. Just for a day."

"You should."

I grabbed two mugs from the cabinet and poured us both coffees. She took hers black. I dumped in a ridiculous amount of cream.

"I keep thinking about that barn," I said, wrapping my hands around the cup. "And how I used to think leaving it meant I'd never get to have parts of me again."

"You were wrong."

"I know."

The coffee was hot against my tongue. I didn't care.

The dog whined and pawed at the screen door. Olivia opened it and let him out, watching as he bounded across the yard toward whatever invisible thing had caught his attention.

"You ever think about leaving here?" I asked.

She looked surprised by the question.

"Sometimes. But not seriously. Not anymore."

"Why?"

She gave me a look like I was asking whether the sky was blue. "Because it's home."

I nodded slowly. Took another sip. Let that word linger on my tongue.

Home.

It didn't pinch anymore. Didn't twist in my stomach like it used to. It wasn't a place I had to escape or a thing someone could deny me. It was this. The morning light. The smell of soap and horses. The sound of a friend shoveling sarcasm across the kitchen table while you drank coffee in your favorite sweatshirt.

I pulled my knees up to the bench and watched the yard through the screen.

I wasn't flawless. Wasn't done. But I wasn't broken either.

And I was mine.

The phone buzzed again. This time, it was a photo.

A chicken.

Wearing a scrunchie.

Standing triumphantly on top of a broom like it had conquered Rome.

I laughed so hard I choked on my coffee. Olivia glanced over, raising an eyebrow, and I shoved the phone at her.

"Oh my god," she said. "That's majestic."

"She said she's naming it Empress Cluck."

"That tracks."

I leaned my head against the wall, still smiling.

I wasn't just surviving anymore. I was living.

And finally, finally, I wanted to.

Eyes that Meet

The air inside Salt City Brews was warm and smelled like roasted espresso beans and cardamom syrup. Not overpowering—just lived in. Familiar in a way I hadn't realized I needed until I stepped through the door. I slid into my usual seat by the window, the high-top with the chipped edge and metal stool which always wobbled to the left. My yellow cardigan went over the back of the chair, and my sketchpad hit the table with a soft thud. I nudged the pencil behind my ear and rolled my shoulders once, slow and loose. No tension curled beneath my collarbones this time. No buzzing under my skin. Just coffee, pencil lead, and the sound of early afternoon chatter humming around me.

The barista behind the counter was new. Not brand new—he'd probably been working here for a few weeks—but I hadn't seen him before. He wore a bandanna tied loosely around his neck and had that calm, distracted look people get when they've memorized every step of their job down to the muscle memory. When he called my name, he didn't even glance up. I liked that. It meant I didn't have to pretend to be anyone else.

I brought the chai back to the table and took a slow sip, letting it coat my mouth and tongue before I set it down. Creamy, sweet, and just enough of a bite. I cracked open the sketchpad and flipped past the filled pages—concepts for the women's wellness space, fabric swatches taped into corners, little doodles of lemon slices and wildflowers whenever I'd been stuck. My fingers paused on a half-finished drawing from two days ago. A living room with floor-to-ceiling windows and a book wall that curved like a spine. I stared at it for a second, then turned the page.

Today wasn't about finishing old things.

Today was for starting new ones.

The next page was blank. No pencil smudges. No eraser marks.

I tapped the graphite tip twice against the page, then started to draw.

I didn't rush it. Didn't overthink the proportions or layout. My hand moved without too much effort, dragging lines across the page in slow, deliberate arcs. A dining space, this time. Cozy but open. Rustic wood table, spindle-back chairs, mismatched but cohesive. I added a tall window off to the side and sketched in the light, soft shading to show where it would hit the edge of the table.

I glanced out the window, watching people move up and down the street. A woman in a long coat pushed a stroller past the window, her mouth tugged up in a tired smile as she glanced toward the café. A couple trailed behind her, deep in conversation, hands brushing but never quite touching.

A guy at the far end of the coffee shop laughed loud enough his table shook. He apologized to the girl across from him, who just rolled her eyes and stole a sip of his drink. There was nothing heavy in it. Nothing forced. Just the sort of moment that passed between people who felt comfortable being exactly where they were.

I turned back to my sketch and added a tea kettle to the table. Not central. Just tucked into the corner, like someone had set it down in the middle of a conversation and forgotten about it.

I glanced at my list next. Five upcoming projects, all small yet meaningful. A nursery, a reading room, a home office for a single mom who worked two jobs and needed the space to feel like hers. I'd promised myself I wouldn't overbook, and I hadn't. But the fact that there was a list at all? That still surprised me.

A few months ago, I'd been terrified to write my name on anything. Now it was printed on contracts, invoices, business cards I hadn't passed out yet but carried in my wallet just in case. Haven and Harmony Interiors wasn't just back—it was growing.

I shifted on the stool, flexed my toes inside my boots. The tension in my shoulders was gone, replaced with a quiet kind of energy that buzzed, low but steady. The kind that came with doing something that mattered. Not to impress someone else or prove I could. Just because it felt right.

I started layering texture into the drawing. A woven rug. Linen napkins. A single chair painted a soft, honeyed yellow. I didn't stop to ask myself why that color kept showing up. It was just part of the way I saw things now.

A shadow passed across the table as someone walked by, and I blinked, realizing how long I'd been sketching. My drink had gone cold. I took a last sip anyway, then leaned back and stretched my arms behind my head until my spine cracked softly.

The pencil smudges on my fingers had gotten darker. I rubbed them absently against the side of my sweatshirt and stared down at the page. It wasn't perfect. The lines weren't all straight. The perspective was a little off on the far window.

But it was beautiful.

Not polished. Not pristine.

Just honest.

The kind of honest that didn't apologize for being warm or soft or full of color.

The kind of honest I'd spent years unlearning—and was finally letting myself believe in again.

I tucked the pencil behind my ear once more and let my fingertips trail across the sketch. The paper felt solid under my hands. Real. I stared at it, taking in every curve and corner, every intentional detail. The scene already looked lived in, like it had been waiting to exist.

The scrape of the stool across the concrete floor barely registered as I shifted, elbow on the table, fingers skimming the page's edge as if it might keep me tethered a little longer. The drawing had taken on weight. Not emotional—just grounded. Like if I reached far enough, I could step inside, run my hand along the windowsill, feel the wood grain beneath my palms. Creation had always carried a charge, but this felt different. There was no urgency, no desperation to prove I was still capable. I just wanted to build something warm. And I had.

The chai was lukewarm now, but I sipped it anyway, letting the sweetness linger on my tongue. Behind me, the grinder whirred—someone ordering a drink with too many adjectives and extra foam. I smirked and tapped the eraser end of my pencil against the tabletop, staring out the wide window facing 300 South.

A man in a firefighter's uniform walked past. Not rushing, not lost in a phone call or barking into a walkie—just walking. His jacket was slung over one shoulder, the dark blue shirt underneath clinging a little to his back like he'd been moving fast earlier. His boots thudded softly against the pavement. I watched without meaning to, the way you notice a flash of yellow among bare branches. Not startling. Just there.

Right before he pushed through the door, he turned his head slightly, glancing back. And his eyes found me.

I didn't flinch. Didn't freeze or look away.

He didn't linger—just a beat, long enough for our gazes to catch and settle. Then he smiled. Not wide. Not flirtatious. Just easy. Like he'd noticed me, and wanted me to know he had.

The bell above the door jingled as it closed behind him, and I exhaled slowly, not realizing I'd been holding onto the breath quite that tightly. I turned my eyes back to my sketchpad. My hand brushed the corner, where the pages curled slightly upward from use.

A smile tugged at my mouth before I could talk myself out of it.

I wasn't going to chase a stranger down the street or write poetry in the margins about blue uniforms and confident grins. I didn't even know his name. Maybe I never would.

But I'd been seen.

And not like before—when being seen meant being picked apart, reshaped, forced into something smaller. This was different. Brief, quiet, nonthreatening. He hadn't tried to claim anything. He'd just... noticed.

My smile widened as I tucked the sketchpad back into my bag. Its edges resisted the zipper, so I slid it in carefully, pulled my cardigan over my shoulders, and stood. The stool scraped again, louder this time, but no one looked up.

I walked to the counter, left my empty cup, nodded at the barista wiping down the espresso machine. Outside, the sun leaned low against the buildings, slanting gold across the sidewalk. I opened the door, stepped into the light, and didn't look back.

My boots clicked against the pavement, each step steady, matching the hum in my chest. No rush. No fear. Just forward.

Epilogue

A Collision of Paths

A Few Months Later

I'D BARELY BEEN SEATED five minutes before the noise swelled to a low roar. Salt City Brews on a Saturday morning wasn't usually my go-to, but I'd promised myself I'd finish this damn proposal by noon, and I needed the structure of ambient chaos to push me through. My old spot near the window was still open, though, and I claimed it like it had my name etched into the wood.

I spread out my notes in controlled chaos—pen uncapped, ruler laid diagonally across the draft page, a color palette swatch resting halfway off the table, just begging to be knocked off. My drink sat safely to the right, steam still curling from the cup. I hadn't even tasted it yet. A soft yellow sweatshirt kept my arms warm despite the industrial chill of the place, and the pencil behind my ear had already left a faint smudge along my temple.

I leaned in, hand hovering over a blank corner of the page, trying to picture how the built-in seating might shift the energy of the room. Everything I wrote had been scribbled, scratched out, and rephrased. The concept was there. It just hadn't landed right yet. My knee bounced under the table.

That's when the table jolted.

Not hard—just enough for the drink to wobble dangerously, a warm splash slipping over the rim. I snapped my head up, startled, blinking once, before I realized it was him.

The firefighter.

The same one who'd glanced back months ago. The same one who hadn't said a word then—just smiled like noticing someone was normal. Expected. Human.

He looked a little stunned, too. Eyes wider than before. Shoulders squared, like he'd brushed against a live wire.

"Oh—shit," he said, already reaching for a napkin from the next table. "Sorry, I didn't see—damn. Did I ruin anything?"

"No, it's fine. It missed the sketch." I lifted the drink to keep it safe from further trauma and gave the table a quick swipe with the napkin he offered.

His eyes lingered on the drawing for half a second, then flicked back to mine.

"Still. Let me get you another. That one's half on your jeans now."

I looked down. A splash of chai had caught the edge of my thigh. It wasn't much, but it was warm, and yeah—it would leave a mark.

"Yeah," I said, giving him a tired grin. "You owe me at least a clean cup for that."

He laughed—low, unforced. "Fair. I'll get you another one. Same order?"

"Chai, extra cardamom."

He nodded, then hesitated, his hand still halfway to his pocket.

"Do you mind if I... sit for a second while they make it? I'll order and come back, I'm not just—trying to crash your morning."

I didn't answer right away. My instinct had always been to wave people off. I liked working alone, liked the silence of being lost in a floorplan. But the way he asked—gentle, almost awkward, like he'd back off if I needed space—made me pause.

"No, you can sit," I said. "If you don't mind the mess."

He smiled again, this time brighter. "Not at all. I'll be right back."

He turned toward the counter, walking like he'd just come off a shift—loose and tired but still alert, like he was used to sudden alarms and half-slept nights. His boots scuffed a little against the concrete floor. I watched until he reached the front of the line.

Then I looked down at the page again, at the smudge of chai along the bottom edge. I didn't brush it off. I just kept staring, that same almost-smile tugging at my lips, waiting to decide what it meant.

He set the fresh chai down carefully, like he didn't quite trust the table not to betray him again. I reached for it, wrapping both hands around the cup and letting the heat settle into my fingers. He sank into the seat across from me, setting his own drink—something dark and serious-looking—on the far side of the table. He didn't say anything right away, just took a breath and let his shoulders drop.

"You always this dangerous in public?" I asked, tilting my head toward the wreckage of the earlier spill. "Spilling drinks, startling strangers."

"Only when I'm off-duty," he said, grinning. "On the clock I'm all grace and coordination."

I laughed, and it didn't sound weird or forced. It came out easy, unguarded. He rested his forearms on the edge of the table, fingers threading loosely together.

"So," he said, nodding toward the sketch. "You an architect or something?"

"Interior designer," I said. "Or, I guess, re-designer? I mostly remodel small spaces. This one's for a reading room attached to a shelter in Sugarhouse."

He leaned in slightly, glancing down at the paper without touching it. "Looks like it's already real."

"I think it wants to be."

It slipped out before I thought it through, but he didn't blink. Just smiled again—slower this time. The kind of smile that wasn't selling anything. "I'm Luke, by the way," he said.

I nodded once. "Honey."

His brows lifted slightly. "Really?"

"Short for Lainey. It's... a long story." I took a sip from the chai. "But it fits now."

"Well. Nice to officially meet you, Honey."

My name sounded different when he said it. Not because of his voice or tone or the way he looked at me, but because I hadn't flinched. I didn't feel like I had to explain myself or brace for some quip. It was just there—out in the open. Mine.

"So, what do you do when you're not almost destroying local businesses?" I asked.

"Rescue cats from trees, mostly." He shrugged. "Drive a giant truck. Nap in awkward chairs at the station. You know, typical hero stuff."

I smirked. "That sounds exhausting."

"It kind of is."

His eyes held mine, and I wasn't trying to be brave or cool—I just didn't look away. He glanced at the sketch, then back at me.

"I like the way you use space," he said. "It's like… it tells you how to breathe."

I blinked at him. I wasn't used to that kind of observation, especially not from a stranger. Or whatever he was now.

"You say that to everyone who draws boxes on paper?"

"Only the ones who look like they're building cathedrals from them."

I didn't know what to do with that, so I laughed again, shook my head, and tucked the pencil back behind my ear. He looked pleased with himself.

"I'm not trying to flirt," he added after a beat. "I mean. I don't know. Maybe I am. But mostly, I just… you seemed like you were in something real, and I was curious."

I let that sit. I didn't have a quick answer. That was new too—being allowed to pause, to feel something without jumping to label it, defend it or cut it off.

"You ever do this before?" I asked.

"What?"

"Talk to random women in coffee shops after spilling drinks on them."

"Nope. First time. Lucky you."

I snorted. "You're not great at this."

"Nope," he said again, grinning.

We both went quiet for a minute. Not awkward—just... letting it settle. I watched a group of students at the door, comparing laptops and laughing too loudly. Behind the counter, a latte machine hissed like a monster. My gaze drifted back to the sketch, then to his hands, resting calmly on the table. Strong hands. A burn scar across one knuckle. No ring. No watch.

"You've got paint on your sleeve," he said.

I looked down. Sure enough, a faded smudge of mustard yellow on my cuff. "Leftover from a client install. Their walls look better than I did walking out."

"Worth it?"

"Every time."

He nodded like he understood that. Maybe he did. Or maybe he just wanted to.

"You wanna hear something dumb?" I asked.

"Always."

"I used to think strength meant staying invisible. Like... if I could keep quiet enough, small enough, I'd survive."

He didn't make a face. Didn't rush to say he understood or relate it back to his own life. He just nodded.

"And now?"

"Now I think strength is just showing up. And not apologizing for it."

"Sounds harder."

"It is." I sipped again. "But better."

He leaned back a little, resting one arm on the top of the chair. "Can I ask what made you switch?"

I stared at the table for a beat too long.

"You don't have to answer," he added quickly.

"I burned a letter," I said quietly. "Not long ago. Everything I ever wanted to say to the guy who made me feel like hiding was survival. I never sent it. I just wanted it out of me."

He watched me carefully, not backing away from the weight of it, but not trying to own it either.

"That's a good reason," he said.

"Yeah."

We fell quiet again. But this time, it was comfortable. Familiar, even. Like he wasn't trying to draw anything out of me. Just make room.

"Do you have a thing for interior designers?" I asked after a beat.

"Only the ones who can kick my ass in spatial planning and make me spill drinks."

I smiled and closed my notebook, setting it aside. I didn't need to finish the proposal right now. It could wait ten more minutes.

He leaned forward, tracing a fingertip along the edge of the napkin I'd used to mop up the spill. His touch didn't reach me, but it felt... patient. Not pushy. Not loaded.

"I'm not looking for anything complicated," I said.

"Neither am I."

"I'm not saying yes to anything, just—"

"I didn't ask anything."

We stared at each other again. He was better at that than I was. But I held my ground this time.

The barista called his name, and he stood slowly.

"Thanks for letting me sit," he said.

I shrugged. "Thanks for not running after I told you I burned a letter like a witch."

He laughed. "I like witches."

He walked to the counter, and I watched him go, something calm unspooling in my chest. When he turned back to wave, I lifted my hand halfway, then let it fall. No promises. No pressure.

Just me. Here. Choosing what stayed, and what left.

I reached for my cup, took a long sip, let the flavor settle deep on my tongue. Then I looked down at the sketch and turned to a new page. I didn't know what I was drawing yet—only that it was mine.

Author's Note

If you made it to this page, thank you.

Honey was never just a story about heartbreak or starting over. It was about survival. About healing. About the quiet, brave moments when you finally choose yourself after years of being made to believe you shouldn't.

Lainey's journey is fictional — but the pain, the silence, the shame, the resilience? That's real for too many people.

This book was written for anyone who's ever been made to feel small by someone who claimed to love them. For anyone who had to leave in pieces and build themselves back slowly, breath by breath, heartbeat by heartbeat.

If that's you, I hope you saw yourself in these pages. I hope you felt seen, felt understood, and above all, I hope you know this:

You are not broken.

You are not too much.

You are not alone.

You are worthy of safety, softness, joy, and love, the kind that never asks you to shrink.

Honey didn't just survive, she came home to herself.

And so can you.

With all my heart,

B. Wiseman

Resources and Support

If *Honey* resonated with you on a personal level—if you've experienced emotional, psychological, financial, or physical abuse—please know this:

You are **not** alone.

You are **not** imagining it.

You are **not** to blame.

And you **deserve** to be safe.

Below are some resources that offer support, shelter, advocacy, and healing for survivors of domestic and intimate partner abuse.

United States

- **National Domestic Violence Hotline**

- 1-800-799-SAFE (7233) | www.thehotline.org

- *Free, confidential support 24/7. Texting and online chat also available.*

- **Love is Respect**

- www.loveisrespect.org | Text "LOVEIS" to 22522

- *Focused on healthy relationships for young adults and teens.*

- **RAINN (Rape, Abuse & Incest National Network)**

- 1-800-656-HOPE (4673) | www.rainn.org

- *Support for survivors of sexual assault and abuse.*

- **Therapy Resources**

- www.psychologytoday.com | www.therapyden.com

- *Find licensed therapists by zip code, specialty, and insurance.*

International Support
- **Canada**: www.sheltersafe.ca
- **UK**: Women's Aid | www.womensaid.org.uk

- **Australia**: 1800RESPECT | www.1800respect.org.au

- **Worldwide Directory**: www.hotpeachpages.net

- *List of crisis centers and helplines in nearly every country.*

There is no one timeline for healing. Whether you are just beginning to find your way out, or years into your journey, you are allowed to take up space. To rest. To speak. To ask for help.

There is strength in softness.

And there is power in beginning again.

Acknowledgments

WRITING *HONEY* WAS A journey of the heart—raw, healing, and deeply personal. I couldn't have done it without the incredible people who walked beside me every step of the way.

To Alex and Fox—this book exists because of you. You held space for me when I couldn't hold it for myself. Your strength, love, and fierce loyalty inspired Olivia's fire, and your belief in me never wavered. Thank you for being my anchors, my light, and my chosen family.

To Kier (Foxlore_art) —thank you for turning a dream into a cover that stopped me in my tracks. Your talent gave *Honey* a visual identity as strong and beautiful as the story itself.

To my editor, beta readers, sensitivity readers, ARC readers, and street team—thank you for pouring your time and hearts into this story. Your encouragement, honesty, and enthusiasm made *Honey* stronger, deeper, and more authentic.

To Jazzy—thank you for being everywhere I needed you, often before I even knew I needed anything. Your help, insight, and kindness shaped so many moments behind the scenes.

To the readers—thank you for picking up *Honey* and trusting me with your time. If this story made you feel something—seen, understood, inspired—then I've done what I came here to do. You are why these stories matter.

To the survivors—*Honey* is for you. For your courage. For your quiet resilience and loud bravery. For the nights you endured and the mornings you rose anyway. May Lainey's story remind you that your past does not define you. You deserve peace, you deserve joy, and you deserve a life that feels like freedom.

WHAT'S NEXT?

COMING SOON: FIREPROOF (BOOK 2 in the Sundust and Smoke Duology)

Lainey didn't expect to find anyone at all—let alone someone like him.

In Fireproof, we follow Lainey's next chapter as her path collides with Luke Matthews, the steady, quiet firefighter she met on an ordinary day in a coffee shop. Their story is one of slow trust, honest healing, and falling in love with safety for the first time.

But love after trauma doesn't come easy. Walls are still up. Fears still whisper.

And fire always leaves something behind.

Fireproof is a story of second chances, new beginnings, and learning how to love when you no longer need to be saved.

About the Author

B is an author who writes stories about resilience, self-discovery, and the complexities of love. From raw, emotional journeys to heart-racing romance, their books explore the strength it takes to heal, grow, and start over. Whether through poetry, fiction, or something in between, B's work resonates with readers who crave deep emotions and unforgettable characters.

Beyond writing, B is passionate about books, fitness, and nutrition. As a certified personal trainer pursuing a career in dietetics, they believe in the power of both mental and physical strength. When they're not crafting compelling stories, you'll find them running their online bookstore, Miles on Paper, supporting indie authors, or working on their next project—whatever form it may take.

Follow B for updates on their latest releases, book recommendations, and behind-the-scenes glimpses into their writing journey.

www.ingramcontent.com/pod-product-compliance
Lightning Source LLC
Chambersburg PA
CBHW060300310726
48976CB00007B/2151